Savannah Spectator Blind Item

Attention all Spectators! Savannah's premier family is about to make headlines again. Last month we told you reporter Jasmine Carmody was about to break a scandalous story involving said family. Now it seems she's canoodling with one of their own! She's been spied on the arm of a trusted, close-as-family friend, even appearing by his side for support when an explosion rocked the family's waterfront headquarters. So it must be love, right?

Or does love depend on what Ms. Carmody writes about the family now that she's almost part of it?

All we can say is between all the weddings, dead bodies, waterfront explosions, bodyguards and other secrets yet to be discovered, Savannah sure is becoming an exciting place to live since a certain millionaire decided to run for the Senate....

Dear Reader,

Welcome back to another passionate month at Silhouette Desire. *A Scandal Between the Sheets* is breaking out as Brenda Jackson pens the next tale in the scintillating DYNASTIES: THE DANFORTHS series. We all love the melodrama and mayhem that surrounds this Southern family— how about you?

The superb Beverly Barton stops by Silhouette Desire with an extra wonderful title in her bestselling series THE PROTECTORS. *Keeping Baby Secret* will keep *you* on the edge of your seat—and curl your toes all at the same time. What would you do if you had to change your name and your entire history? Sheri WhiteFeather tackles that compelling question when her heroine is forced to enter the witness protection program in *A Kept Woman*. Seems she was a kept woman of another sort, as well…so be sure to pick up this fabulous read if you want the juicy details.

Kristi Gold has written the final, fabulous installment of THE TEXAS CATTLEMAN'S CLUB: THE STOLEN BABY series with *Fit for a Sheikh*. (But don't worry, we promise those sexy cattlemen with be back.) And rounding out the month are two wonderful stories filled with an extra dose of passion: Linda Conrad's dramatic *Slow Dancing With A Texan* and Emilie Rose's supercharged *A Passionate Proposal*.

Enjoy all we have to offer this month—and every month— at Silhouette Desire.

Melissa Jeglinski

Melissa Jeglinski
Senior Editor, Silhouette Desire

Please address questions and book requests to:
Silhouette Reader Service
U.S.: 3010 Walden Ave., P.O. Box 1325, Buffalo, NY 14269
Canadian: P.O. Box 609, Fort Erie, Ont. L2A 5X3

DYNASTIES: THE DANFORTHS

SCANDAL BETWEEN THE SHEETS

BRENDA JACKSON

Published by Silhouette Books
America's Publisher of Contemporary Romance

Special thanks and acknowledgment are given to
Brenda Jackson for her contribution to the
DYNASTIES: THE DANFORTHS series.

A good name is to be chosen rather than great riches,
loving favor rather than silver and gold.
—Proverbs 22:1

This book is dedicated to my editor, Mavis Allen.
Thanks for all that you do!

 SILHOUETTE BOOKS

ISBN 0-373-76573-8

SCANDAL BETWEEN THE SHEETS

Visit Silhouette at www.eHarlequin.com

Printed in U.S.A.

Books by Brenda Jackson

Silhouette Desire

Delaney's Desert Sheikh #1473
A Little Dare #1533
Thorn's Challenge #1552
Scandal Between the Sheets #1573

BRENDA JACKSON

is a die "heart" romantic who married her childhood sweetheart and still proudly wears the "going steady" ring he gave her when she was fifteen. Because she's always believed in the power of love, Brenda's stories always have happy endings. In her real-life love story, Brenda and her husband of thirty years live in Jacksonville, Florida, and have two sons in college.

An award-winning author of ten romance titles, Brenda divides her time between family, writing and working in management at a major insurance company. You may write Brenda at P.O. Box 28267, Jacksonville, Florida 32226, or visit her Web site at www.brendajackson.net.

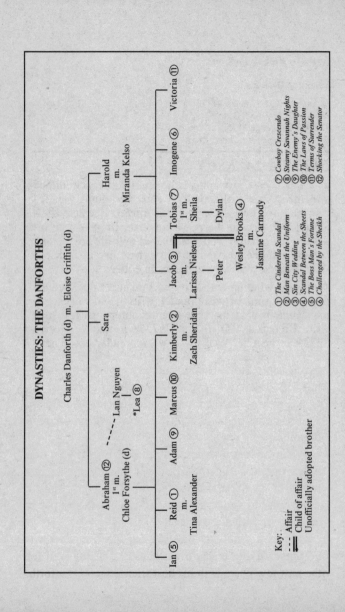

DYNASTIES: THE DANFORTHS

Charles Danforth (d) m. Eloise Griffith (d)

Sara

Harold
m.
Miranda Kelso

Abraham ⑫
1ˢᵗ m.
Chloe Forsythe (d)

Lan Nguyen

*Lea ⑧

Reid ①   Adam ⑨   Marcus ⑩   Kimberly ②
m.   m.
Tina Alexander   Zach Sheridan

Ian ⑤

Jacob ③   Tobias ⑦
m.   1ˢᵗ m.
Larissa Nielsen   Sheila

Peter   Dylan

Wesley Brooks ④
m.
Jasmine Carmody

Imogene ⑥   Victoria ⑪

Key:
- - - Affair
═══ Child of affair
Unofficially adopted brother

① The Cinderella Scandal
② Man Beneath the Uniform
③ Sin City Wedding
④ Scandal Between the Sheets
⑤ The Boss Man's Fortune
⑥ Challenged by the Sheikh

⑦ Cowboy Crescendo
⑧ Steamy Savannah Nights
⑨ The Enemy's Daughter
⑩ The Laws of Passion
⑪ Terms of Surrender
⑫ Shocking the Senator

One

Wesley Brooks yawned away sleep as he pulled on his jeans, deciding to investigate the noise that had awakened him. A quick glance at the clock on his nightstand showed it was a little past one in the morning. His flight from Dallas to Savannah had been delayed due to thunderstorms and when he had finally arrived home he had quickly showered then collapsed onto the bed.

When he had first heard the noise it had taken him a few minutes to get his bearings and remember just where he was. He had moved into this house only a week before leaving to go out of town for a couple of days on important business.

He had to blink several times to recall that he was no longer living at the town house he had shared for the past few years with his best friend, Jacob Danforth.

Jake, the fun-loving, party animal, was now happily married to Larissa and was the father to a precious little boy name Peter. Deciding to give the newlyweds privacy, Wesley had moved out and purchased his dream home, a beautiful, old and prestigious house on the Savannah River.

Wesley heard another sound.

Not bothering to put on any shoes, he quietly slipped down the stairs to investigate, pretty sure at this point that he was not just hearing things. When he got to the bottom of the stairs he heard the noise again and quickly determined it was coming from the outside.

He opened the French doors and stepped out onto the terrace. It was April and spring was in the air. A full moon glowed in the sky and cast a shimmer of light across the landscaped yard where his garbage cans sat.

Remembering that he had failed to lock the security gate when he had come home, he quickly concluded the noise was probably a stray dog or cat trying to find scraps to eat. Wesley was about to turn around and go back inside when he saw the movement of a figure that was too large to be an animal of the four-legged kind.

His gaze sharpened as he watched someone hunched over his garbage cans rummaging through them. Immediately he felt a deep stirring in his heart for anyone that poverty-stricken. Thanks to the success of his Internet company he made millions, but the one thing he made a point of *not* doing was forgetting where he'd come from—although after thirty years the memory was pretty foggy in his mind. All he knew was that at the age of three months, he had been left on the doorstep of an orphanage and grew up being bounced from foster home to foster home. At the age of fourteen he had run away and had lived on the streets for three days before the police had found him. During those three days, a homeless old man by the name of Al Lombard had befriended him. Wesley had discovered that Al had once been a teacher in the school system and after losing his wife in a tragic house fire, with no family, close friends or insurance, he had fallen on hard times.

It was Al who had shared his food with him; Al who had shared his blankets at night so he could stay warm; and Al who had helped to keep him safe. To this very day he appreciated Al's kindness. As soon as Wesley had made his first million, he had hired a private investigator to find Al, only to discover the man had died of pneumonia the year before.

Bringing his thoughts back to the present, Wesley made a quick decision to offer this homeless person enough money to enjoy a decent meal someplace, as well as a warm place to spend the night. That was the least he could do. Quietly going back inside the house, he raced up the stairs to grab a few dollars from his wallet, hoping the person would still be there when he returned.

Some reporters will do just about anything for a story and I have become one of them.

That thought floated through Jasmine Carmody's mind as she continued looking through Wesley

Brooks's garbage. You could learn a lot about a person by going through their trash, but so far the only thing she'd been able to discover about Wesley Brooks, dot.com millionaire and Savannah's number one player, was that he loved spaghetti, the microwave kind. What about the kind you made from scratch? Hadn't any of his numerous lady friends discovered that the way to most men's hearts was through their stomach and not necessarily that part of their anatomy that was located below the belt?

But then, if rumors were true, Wesley Brooks wasn't like most men. She had read his bio enough times to know the full story…at least what there was of it. He'd been an orphan and had bounced back and forth from foster homes until he was sixteen. It was while he had been attending high school that he had struck up a close friendship with Jacob Danforth of the prominent Savannah Danforths.

Jacob and Wesley became the best of friends and when Wesley was about to be sent to yet another foster home, Jacob's parents, Harold and Miranda Danforth, stepped in and offered Wesley a home and a chance for stability in his life for the remainder of his high-school years, becoming the first family he'd ever known. When it came time for college, Wesley's proficiency in sports and his talent for math got him a scholarship to Georgia Tech University. Jacob Danforth also attended Georgia Tech and the two roomed together for the four years they were there.

Jasmine sighed as she continued to dig through the garbage. There wasn't too much about Wesley Brooks that she didn't know including the fact that the Internet-based restaurant supply business he'd created a few years ago had made him millions, and at the age of thirty he was considered one of the wealthiest men in Savannah—as well as one of the most sought after bachelors. She also knew about his close relationship to the Danforth family, which was the main reason she was digging through his garbage at this ungodly hour.

Jasmine suddenly went still. For a panicked moment, she'd thought she had heard something. When seconds passed and she didn't hear a thing, she continued with what she was doing.

According to Veronica "Ronnie" Strongman, a fellow reporter and one of her closest friends, being home on a Saturday night was a no-no for Wesley Brooks. He was somewhere doing what she'd read he did best…besides managing his business…and that was playing the role of millionaire playboy.

She stopped upon hearing another sound and turned around. She swallowed a scream when her gaze collided with that of the playboy millionaire himself. The sight of him took her breath away and when he walked out of the shadows barefoot and wearing only his jeans, her gaze first locked on his bare chest before moving upward to his gorgeous hazel eyes. He was taller than she had imagined and very solid, all muscles and no fat. He had chestnut-colored skin, the kind that didn't make you think of open fires, but stirring up a different kind of fire.

She had been caught red-handed in Wesley Brooks's trash and the first thought that came to her mind was to run. But for some reason, she couldn't move. She felt glued to the spot.

*   *   *

Wesley was shocked. What he thought was a "he" had turned out to be a "she." He saw the panic in the woman's eyes and knew she was about to take off running but he couldn't let her go without first offering her something. A part of him wondered what had happened in her young life to leave her this destitute.

"Wait! Don't go. I want to help."

He watched her eyes widen and thought she had the most incredible dark brown eyes that he had ever seen on a woman. A scarf completely covered her head and here in the darkened corner of the yard where only the moonlight shone through, he could see that her features were just as incredible as her eyes. Her skin tone was the color of rich cocoa and she appeared to be no more than twenty-five; the same age he had been when he had made his first millions.

She was wearing what appeared to be a well-worn jogging suit and surprisingly, she smelled good. His practiced nostrils recognized the fragrance, one that had an alluring scent. This particular brand would normally be too costly for a penniless person's taste. Evidently, she'd hit gold in someone's garbage and had come upon a half-empty bottle of some woman's expensive perfume.

He blinked, forcing his mind to concentrate on the situation at hand and not on the possibilities, since, as far as he was concerned, there weren't any. "How old are you?" he asked quietly, not wanting to scare her and wanting to assure her that he meant her no harm, although she was trespassing on his property.

He watched as she took a step back and when she

did so, he was able to see more of her and suddenly, he could barely breathe. There was something about her that pulled on his heartstrings deeper than before. There was no way she should have to resort to this type of life for herself.

"I'm twenty-six," she finally said, regaining his absolute attention. "Why?"

"I just wanted to know. Here's some money," he said, offering the wad of cash he held in his hand. "This is probably about five hundred dollars. Take it and go get something to eat and keep the rest to take care of yourself," he said, thinking she wasn't doing such a bad job of that anyway. She managed to look a lot more decent than some other homeless women.

"And since you won't find too many fast-food places open this late at night, if you're real hungry I can fix you something to eat."

He watched her lips twitch into a smile when she said, "A microwave spaghetti dinner?"

Wesley blinked, then comprehended what she had said and why she had said it. He couldn't help throwing his head back and letting out a hearty laugh. Evidently she had discovered that hitting his garbage cans had been a complete waste of her time. It was a known fact among his friends just how much he liked spaghetti. When he wasn't dining at some elegant and expensive restaurant, the microwave dinners were pretty damn satisfying, as well as filling.

By the time he had brought his laughter under control he saw she had taken off, and the only thing he could see was a flash of her jogging suit as she sprinted down his driveway and slipped out of the decorative wrought iron gate. "Hey, stop! Wait! Don't leave without taking the money!"

Too late, he thought, as he watched her fleeing back. Careful of his bare feet, he walked part of the way down his driveway to see what direction she had gone but didn't see anything. It was as if she had totally disappeared. Feeling disgusted that he had scared her off before she had taken the money he'd offered, he was about to turn to go back inside the house when he happened to glance down. There was something lying on the concrete and glittering in the moonlight. Reaching down he picked it up and saw it was some sort of a locket the woman had evidently dropped. Clenching it firmly in the palm of his hand, Wesley went back into the house.

The moment Jasmine was inside her apartment she leaned against the door and tried to slow down her heart rate as she let out a deep sigh of relief. That had been close, too close, and the very thought that Wesley Brooks had assumed she was a homeless person was almost too much.

What was he doing home on a Saturday night?

Ronnie had tipped her off that Wesley Brooks had repaired Abraham Danforth's computer rather recently, and Jasmine had decided to go through his garbage just in case he had tossed out anything of interest on Abraham. Abraham Danforth had announced his candidacy for senator a few months ago and since then she had been trying to get a breaking-newsworthy story. No one could be as squeaky clean as Abraham Danforth wanted everyone to believe he was, and if there was dirt to be found, she intended to be the one to find it. She desperately needed to break a big story if she wanted to advance her career as a newspaper reporter. By making a name for herself she could pursue bigger opportunities.

Wesley Brooks hadn't had a clue why she had been going through his trash and she was grateful for that. Had he known she was a newspaper reporter, he could have charged her with trespassing among other things, especially since he had a sign posted on his property that clearly said, No Trespassing. She was glad she had parked her car around the corner, a good distance from his house. Although by the time she had reached her vehicle she had been out of breath, at least he hadn't tried following her.

And to think he had offered her five hundred dollars! She shook her head, shocked. The playboy millionaire had a heart. A big heart. He had even offered to share his food with her, and Jasmine knew she had seen a side of Wesley Brooks that very few people saw. It appeared that when it came to the less fortunate, he had a caring spirit and a part of her couldn't help but be touched by it.

She sighed, thinking she had really gotten desperate to be going through people's garbage. With her inability to uncover dirt on Abraham, she had decided to delve into the personal lives of the second generation of Danforths to see what muck she could dig up on them, as well.

Last month, she thought she had just the story on Abraham Danforth's nephew, Jacob Danforth. She had discovered that a woman, Larissa Neilson, had given

birth to his baby two years ago. However, the woman
had decided to tell Jacob the truth before he found out
about his child by reading it in the papers. When Jacob
had found out he had a son, he had quickly done the
right thing by stepping in and marrying Larissa. As a
result he had destroyed the opportunity for Jasmine to
blow the story wide open. So now she wasn't sure just
what angle she wanted to use to get the most effect
when she eventually wrote the story.

She crossed the room and stopped beside the telephone, tempted to call Ronnie and chew her out for
giving her wrong information. Evidently, Mr. Brooks
had changed his routine and decided to stay in tonight.
But then Jasmine couldn't discount the possibility that
a female friend could have been waiting for him in
bed. She wouldn't put anything past someone who was
as gorgeous as he was, and tonight, even with just the
moonlight overhead, she had managed to get an eye-
ful.

Wesley Brooks was a good-looking man. She had
seen his photographs a number of times but tonight
was the first time she had seen him in the flesh, and,
boy, what flesh it was.

She blushed, not believing where her thoughts had
gone and decided, what the hell, she might as well get
it out of her system, although she knew that would be
impossible. The sight of him barefoot and wearing
nothing but a pair of jeans would be permanently
etched on her mind.

He was sexy as hell, powerfully built and had a
body like male bodies were supposed to look. His
shoulders were muscular, sleek, and his chest was

broad, muscled with a patch of sparse dark hair that trailed all the way past the waistline of his jeans.

Instead of taking off when she had first seen him, she had stood rooted in place, her mind frozen, and her heart thumping so strongly she'd been barely able to catch her breath. Her body still burned thinking about it. Nothing like this had ever happened to her before. For the past few years she had been too busy trying to make a name for herself as a reporter, chasing leads to possible breaking stories, that she had forgotten that she was a woman who could appreciate a good-looking man when she saw one.

Too bad the man had been Wesley Brooks. She wondered if he saw her again as Jasmine Carmody, newspaper reporter for the *Savannah Morning News*, would he recognize her? If he did, he would definitely be angry when he put two and two together, but she couldn't think about that now. The only thing she wanted to think about was taking a shower and going to bed.

Once she got to the bathroom, she turned on the water full blast and began stripping out of her clothes and removing the scarf from her head. Moments later, she pulled the mass of braids that flowed to her shoulders, back away from her face and stepped beneath the shower. Her head fell back as the warm, pulsating water ran down her face, throat, neck, pounding her shoulders and loosening her muscles as it flowed down the rest of her body, washing away her tension. She slowly began to feel relaxed, clean and soothed.

Stepping out of the shower a while later, she quickly grabbed a huge towel and began drying off, appreciating that tomorrow was Sunday, the only day she kept for herself. She would attend early-morning church service and then as expected, she would put in an appearance at her father's home and tolerate her stepmother, Evelyn, and stepsisters, Alyssa and Mallory's, unpleasantness.

She wondered what aspect of herself they would pick on tomorrow. Would they still harp on the fact that in their opinion she was too thin and needed to gain weight? Or would they discuss her inability to find a man just because she never brought one to dinner?

That both Alyssa and Mallory never invited a man to dinner, either, was beside the point. Her life was the one that got scrutinized and criticized. Both her stepsisters were spoiled, but Evelyn seemed to overlook that. At twenty-four Alyssa was still living at home and Mallory, at twenty-two, had moved into an apartment that Jasmine knew for certain her father was paying for since Mallory was unemployed. Jasmine was the only self-supporting one in the bunch yet she was never good enough.

She remembered how things had been before Evelyn and her daughters had entered her and her father's lives. Her mother had died when she was nine and for five years there had been just her and her father. Then one day Dr. James Carmody announced he was remarrying and that his new wife was a single woman with two young girls. He had excitedly exclaimed that the five of them would become a happy blended family, just like on *The Brady Bunch*.

He had been dead wrong. No sooner had Evelyn

changed her name and moved in, than things began changing for the worse. She made it obvious that Alyssa and Mallory came first in everything, except chores. They had been the ones pampered and Jasmine had been the one left doing anything and everything they didn't want to do. It never did any good to complain. It only made matters worse for her.

Sadly to say, her father had always spent a lot of his time at the hospital taking care of patients, and when he'd finally noticed what was happening in his home, it was too late. The damage had been done. The only good thing was that Jasmine knew her father loved her. He had immediately tried to set matters right and at one time had gone so far as to threaten to divorce Evelyn if he ever discovered she was mistreating Jasmine again.

Jasmine knew that one word from her and Evelyn and her daughters would be history. And as much as they weren't her favorite people, she didn't want to think of them being put out on the streets. Without her father's name and money, the three women would be like fish out of water. So the majority of the time Jasmine never bothered to tell him how Evelyn and her daughters continued to mistreat her. Instead, she tried to make the best of the situation and only went to visit them once a week on Sundays for dinner.

Jasmine smiled when she thought about her mother and what a warm, loving individual she had been. After her mother's death, there had been Aunt Rena, her mother's sister who had always been there for her until she had died the summer Jasmine turned twenty-one. It was that summer when Aunt Rena had given her a box containing her mother's personal belongings. They were items that Jasmine's father had given Aunt Rena for safekeeping. Evidently, James Carmody had known that if Evelyn ever got her hands on any of it, she would have given them to her daughters instead.

Jasmine had appreciated her father's thoughtfulness in looking out for her that way and in protecting the precious gifts her mother had wanted her to have. Most of the items had been jewelry that had been passed down through at least four generations—rare, expensive jewelry.

The piece that had caught Jasmine's heart more than anything had been the beautiful gold-domed embossed locket she always remembered her mother wearing. From the day her aunt Rena had given it to her, the locket had been a constant companion around her neck. She never took it off and it served as a reminder of a time when she had been deeply loved by both of her parents.

Automatically, she reached for it, where it usually rested between her breasts and suddenly went still when she discovered it wasn't there. Frantically, she went to the laundry hamper to pull out the jogging outfit she'd been wearing tonight, in hopes the locket may have slipped from around her neck and fallen inside her clothes. She had gotten the clasp on the locket repaired just last year.

When Jasmine couldn't find it in the house she then slipped on a bathrobe and went outside to retrace her steps to her car, as well as going through every inch of her vehicle. She still found nothing. Jasmine knew the only other place it could possibly be was somewhere on Wesley Brooks's property. She became distraught at the possibility that it could have fallen in his trash while she'd been going through it.

Reentering her house, Jasmine slumped back against the door as tears filled her eyes. That locket meant everything to her and now it was gone. If it were on Wesley Brooks's property, how would she get it back? If he thought his property was open to trespassers after what happened tonight, chances were he would take precautions and lock the security gates the next time he was out.

And what if he found her locket? Would he think that perhaps it belonged to one of his lady friends and assume that no homeless person could own anything of such value?

Crossing the room, Jasmine slumped down in a chair wondering what in the world she was going to do? The last thing she wanted was to encounter the likes of Wesley Brooks again, but now it appeared that she had no choice.

The next day Wesley stood on his terrace and inhaled the fresh morning air with a cup of coffee in one hand and the locket he had found the night before in the other. He frowned as he carefully studied the piece of jewelry. He wasn't an expert but he'd bet anything the item was worth a fortune. As he took a sip of coffee he knew there was only one way to find out. Bruce Crawford.

He and Bruce had met a few years ago and the man's expertise in unique custom jewelry sales and designs was well known. Wesley had a feeling the piece of jewelry he was looking at was a very rare piece. He had pondered why a homeless person would have such a piece of jewelry in their possession without exchanging it for money to buy food for most of the night. Then he had opened the locket and found his answer when he saw that the picture inside bore a striking likeness to the destitute woman who had been going through his garbage. He had quickly surmised that the woman in the locket was the young woman's mother and she had kept the locket for sentimental reasons. He couldn't help but admire her for making such a sacrifice and was determined to see that the locket was returned to her.

He shook his head, not understanding his need to see the woman again and to make sure that she was all right. The shadows beneath his eyes indicated he'd spent a sleepless night thinking about her. It had been a long time since any woman had made him lose sleep. But there had been something about her, something he couldn't put his finger on that had appealed to him on an emotional level. He couldn't push from his mind the memory of the smile that had touched her lips when he'd offered her food, and couldn't help wondering what had brought her to such a poverty-stricken state.

Hearing the telephone ring, Wesley went back inside and, after placing his coffee cup on the counter, picked up the phone. "Yes?"

"You haven't forgotten about the card game tomorrow night, have you?"

Wesley chuckled upon hearing the sound of Ian Danforth's voice. Ian was Abraham Danforth's oldest

son, and since Abraham and Harold Danforth were
brothers, Ian was also Jake's cousin. When Abraham
had declared his candidacy for the senate, Ian took
over the reins of the family company, Danforth and
Danforth. Since Ian had been in charge of things, he
had significantly increased the company's profits by
creating a coffee import business. Ian was also a silent
but equal partner with his younger brother Adam and
his cousin Jake in a very successful joint venture—
Danforth & Danforth's chain of upscale coffeehouses.

"No, I haven't forgotten. Have you talked to Jake
and the others?"

"Yes and even Dad mentioned he would be stop-
ping by."

Wesley raised a dark brow. In all the years that he
and the Danforth males had been playing cards together, Abraham Danforth had never put in an appearance. On the other hand, Harold would drop by
occasionally to join the game.

Ian must have read his thoughts because at that moment he said, "Surprised the hell out of me, too. But
then I guess running for the senate means you have to
start playing the role of devoted father," Ian said
somewhat bitterly.

Wesley knew that all of Abraham's children—Ian,
Adam, Reid, Marcus and Kimberly—had nothing but
unhappy memories of a strict and cheerless childhood
that had mainly been spent at boarding schools after
their mother had died. They had spent most of their
holidays with their uncle Harold, who became a father
figure to them, and the only reason they had agreed to
rally to support their father in his bid for the senate

was because Harold, who they all adored, had asked them to.

Because Wesley had also lived in Harold and Miranda's home, he and Abraham's five children, as well as Harold and Miranda's four—Jake, Tobias, Imogene and Victoria—had grown up close and fiercely loyal to each other.

Wesley then thought about Victoria, Harold and Miranda's youngest daughter. Five years ago at the age of seventeen she had been reported missing. Although the Danforths had never given up the search to find her, the police had closed the case on her disappearance.

"I'll see you tomorrow night. Come ready to lose your money," Wesley said.

"Like hell I will," Ian said laughing as they ended their conversation.

Wesley hung up the phone smiling. His smile faded when he noticed that he was still holding the locket. A part of him would not be satisfied until he returned it to its owner.

Veronica Strongman watched as Jasmine paced back and forth in her living room, obviously clearly agitated. "Walking a hole in the floor won't help, Jazz," Ronnie decided to say moments later when Jasmine continued her pacing.

Jasmine stopped and met Ronnie's gaze. "I want that big break, Ronnie, and I believe the Danforths will give it to me. Think of everything that has happened since Abraham Danforth kicked off his campaign— the corpse of a young woman was discovered during

renovations at the Danforth family mansion, as well
as me finding out that Jacob Danforth had a love child.
But so far neither has turned into the earth-shattering
story that I'm looking for. Then I hear about Abraham
Danforth's computer getting repaired, hoping to gather
something from that, I still come up with nothing.''

Jasmine slumped down on the sofa. ''And then to
top things off, I've lost the most precious thing I've
ever owned. That locket means everything to me and
I want it back.''

Ronnie nodded. ''Chances are it's somewhere on
Wesley Brooks's property and he hasn't seen it yet.''

Jasmine raised hopeful eyes to her friend. ''You
think so?''

''Yes, and all you have to do is find out the next
time he won't be home.''

Jasmine sighed deeply. ''What if he locks his gate
this time?''

Ronnie waved her hand in a dismissive gesture.
''Chances are he won't. I suggest that we figure out
the times he won't be at home, with a little more ac-
curacy than before, then go back and search the
grounds for it. I'll even help you.''

Jasmine's face lit into a smile, the first since she
had gone to her father's house for dinner earlier that
day. ''Thanks, Ronnie. I won't be able to get a good
night's sleep until my locket is back around my neck
where it belongs.''

Two

Wesley tossed aside the papers he had been reading when the buzzer sounded on his desk. He quickly picked up the phone. "Yes, Melinda, what is it?"

"Sorry for the interruption, Mr. Brooks, but you asked that I put Bruce Crawford through the minute he called."

Wesley sat up straight in his chair. He had spoken with Crawford only yesterday. Was it too much to hope that he had gotten a lead already? "Thanks, Melinda, please put him through." He took a long swallow of coffee while he waited for his secretary to make the connection.

"Bruce?" he said, when the man's booming voice came on the line. "You're calling back already?"

"Yes, and next time give me something harder to

do. What you wanted was a piece of cake. I knew it the moment I saw that locket.''

Relief coursed through Wesley making him grin. ''I'll remember that the next time. So what did you find out?''

''Basically just what I told you yesterday. That locket is an heirloom dated back to the early eighteen hundreds, pure gold. The style is…''

Wesley wasn't interested in the style of the locket. He wanted to know anything Bruce could tell him about the owner. ''What about the person who owns the locket?'' he interrupted by asking. ''Could you find out anything about her?''

Bruce chuckled. ''As a matter of fact, yes. I noticed the clasp had been replaced. There are a limited number of jewelers who would work on a piece this valuable. It seems that same locket was taken to a jeweler for repair of the clasp about a year ago. Luckily the man who owns the repair shop still had the paperwork. The owner of the locket is a woman by the name of Jasmine Carmody.''

Wesley frowned, wondering where had he heard that name before. ''Jasmine Carmody?''

''Yes, Jasmine Carmody, and I have her address if you need it.''

Wesley lifted a brow. ''She has an address?''

Bruce chuckled again. ''Of course she has an address. She has to live someplace, doesn't she?''

Not necessarily, Wesley started to say since most homeless people didn't reside in any one place. But instead he said. ''Yes, I suppose. So what address do you have for her?''

Again Wesley was taken aback when Bruce rattled off Jasmine Carmody's address. It belonged to a very upscale apartment complex off Abercorn Street in downtown Savannah. "Are you sure this is the correct address?"

"That's the address indicated on the work-order invoice. I was able to get a copy of it and I'm looking at it as we speak. There's even a home telephone number, as well as a business number and mobile number."

Wesley began rubbing the back of his neck, suddenly feeling tension building there. None of what Bruce was telling him made any sense. Why would a homeless person be living in an upscale apartment and have home, business and mobile phones? "Would you give me those numbers, please?"

Without asking any questions, Bruce provided him with the information. "Anything else you want to know, Wes?"

This is one that I'll have to figure out on my own, Wesley thought. "No, that's about it. I appreciate all the information you were able to find out. I owe you one, Bruce." A few minutes later, he and the other man ended their conversation.

Wesley leaned back in his chair and studied the address and the phone numbers he had written down. It seemed that his mystery lady was becoming more mysterious by the minute. It also seemed his mystery lady was not homeless.

Carmody? Now where had he heard that last name before? He remembered attending a charity benefit once and meeting a Dr. James Carmody, a well-known orthopedic surgeon in the city. He also remembered meeting the man's wife and two daughters. Mrs. Carmody had all but shoved her daughters in Wesley's face, letting him know the two young women were ripe for marriage if he was interested.

He hadn't been interested then and he wasn't interested now. Marriage was definitely the last thing on his mind, although he had to admit that Jake seemed pretty damn happy with it. It still amazed him that his best friend could so easily slip into the role of father and husband like he was made for it.

Thinking of his friend made Wesley recall that Jake had also been in attendance at the charity benefit that night. Jake was better at remembering the names of people than he was, so maybe he ought to run the name by Jake and…

Something suddenly clicked in Wesley's mind: a conversation he'd had with Jake and Larissa just a few weeks ago when they'd told him about a newspaper reporter who had been the one to find out about Jake being the father of Larissa's three-year-old son, Peter. The reporter had threatened to blow the story wide open. Since Jake hadn't known he had a son, Larissa had done the smart thing in going straight to Jake before he had a chance to read it in the newspapers.

Jake had immediately done the honorable thing and asked Larissa to marry him. She'd been reluctant at first, but then she had eventually agreed that it was in the best interest of their son for her and Jake to marry. What might have begun as a marriage of convenience between Jake and Larissa was now a marriage of love.

There was no doubt in Wesley's mind that his best friend was deeply in love with his wife.

Again, Wesley racked his brain as to where he had heard the name Jasmine Carmody before. He seemed to remember that the reporter who had dug into Jake and Larissa's past had been named Jasmine something.

Deciding to solve the puzzle once and for all, he picked up the phone and placed a call to Jake. Less than ten minutes after talking to Jake, Wesley was slamming the phone down in anger. The woman who'd had the nerve to trespass on his property and rummage through his garbage was not a homeless person. In fact she was a long way from being penniless and probably didn't know the meaning of being destitute. But worst of all was the knowledge that Jasmine Carmody was a reporter and he outright despised reporters. She had played on his kindness and had made a complete fool out of him.

He stood and crossed the room to the window and gazed out, trying to calm his anger. No matter how many times he saw it, he thought Savannah's riverfront was breathtaking. What had once been a row of cotton warehouses was now a plaza that consisted of shops, restaurants and offices. He had been smart enough to know the value of investing in waterfront property for both his business and personal use.

His thoughts shifted back to Jasmine Carmody. The woman had actually been going through his garbage looking for something she could use in her campaign to discredit Abraham Danforth. In his opinion that made her nothing more than a self-serving piranha of a reporter.

She didn't care who she hurt as long as she got her story, and from what he'd seen the other night, it appeared she would go to any lengths to get it. Just what had she hoped to find? Even if he had something he wanted kept confidential, did she think he would have been stupid enough to toss it in the garbage?

He couldn't stop his thoughts from drifting back to his college days and thinking of Caroline Perry. Caroline was a journalism student he had dated while a member of the Georgia Tech football team. He had really cared for her and would even go so far as to say he had actually loved her. But he had found out too late that love had been the farthest thing from Caroline's mind and all she had wanted from him was a story. She'd been interested only in breaking a story on steroid use by the football team. He had been devastated when he learned she'd only been using him. She had taken the information that he had shared with her in strict confidence and had written an article for the school newspaper. In the end, he had gotten kicked off the football team and was shunned by his teammates. Since then, he'd never trusted another reporter, and as far as women were concerned, he would love them and leave them. He would never give his heart to another woman again.

He walked back to his desk. Jasmine Carmody had made a grave mistake. She would find out the hard way that no one, and he meant no one, made a fool of Wesley Brooks.

Talk about close calls again, Jasmine thought as she let herself into her apartment. She and Ronnie had gone over to Wesley Brooks's home during their lunch hour, only to find he had locked the gate.

Determined to get onto his property anyway, she had attempted to climb the massive wrought-iron gate only to hear Ronnie's warning moments later that someone was coming. She had barely made it back down safely to the ground, and she and Ronnie had hightailed it to the nearest bushes, when Wesley Brooks had pulled up in his vintage red Corvette. How were they to know that he would be coming home for lunch? And then when he had leaned out of the vehicle to punch in the numbers to open his security gate, he had glanced around as if he had known she was out there somewhere hiding, which was ridiculous. There was no way he could have known since like the last time, she had parked her car out of sight.

Jasmine tossed her purse on the sofa and went into the kitchen feeling totally frustrated. She and Ronnie had come pretty close to being discovered. Millionaire or no millionaire, why couldn't the man have a schedule that they could figure out? He had a tendency to appear when you least expected him.

She was about to take some leftover lasagna out of the freezer when she heard the phone ring. She decided to let the answering machine pick it up just in case it was Evelyn or one of her stepsisters. There was no way she could deal with any of them right now.

She had just closed her freezer door when the deep, husky timbre of a male's voice floated across the living room and reached her alert ears all the way in the kitchen.

"Good evening, Ms. Carmody, this is Wesley

Brooks. I believe I have something of yours and if you're interested in getting it back, I suggest that you meet me tonight at seven o'clock at the original D&D Coffeehouse. The decision to show up is strictly up to you.'' The phone clicked loudly when he abruptly ended the call.

Jasmine stood shell-shocked, rooted in place. She could hear the sound of blood rushing fast and furious to her brain. Wesley Brooks knew who she was and had found her locket. And from the sound of it, although his voice had remained rather calm, she had picked up on more than a tinge of anger in his tone. The man was definitely not a happy camper.

A shiver lapped at her nerve endings as she glanced down at her watch. He wanted them to meet tonight at seven and it was almost six now. The first thought that came to her mind was not to go, but then she knew if she didn't show up she might as well kiss her locket goodbye and she couldn't do that. Right now he was holding the ace and evidently he knew how to play it.

She sighed deeply, wondering what sort of explanation she could give him that would sound plausible as to why she had been on his property that night, then quickly decided there wasn't one. The bottom line was that she had trespassed and had been going through his garbage. Hell, he had caught her red-handed and she'd been careless enough to leave evidence behind.

She wondered how on earth he had traced the locket back to her and decided it really didn't matter. Besides, she didn't have time to ponder the question of how she had gotten caught, not if she wanted to meet him at the time he had mandated in his phone call.

As she put the lasagna back in the freezer, she headed toward her bedroom. She would take a shower, get dressed and leave to meet the one man she had hoped to never see again.

Wesley checked his watch. Jasmine Carmody had less than five minutes to show her face. He hoped she would be on time because the last thing he felt toward her was tolerance. She had already pushed the wrong buttons with him and he wouldn't suggest that she tried pushing any more.

Although he hadn't seen her again since that night, he had a feeling that she had shown up on his property sometime today, right before he had come home for lunch. When he had rolled down the window to punch in the numbers to open his security gate, he had noticed the footprints in his flower bed.

Evidently she'd come looking for the locket and had been highly disappointed to discover his gate locked. He was glad he had thought to secure it that morning before he'd left. Otherwise Ms. Carmody would have taken the liberty to snoop again. Well, she was going to find out tonight that she had sniffed around one time too many. He was intent on teaching her a lesson that she would never forget.

He glanced toward the entrance of the coffeehouse the moment she walked in. Even minus the scarf that she'd worn on her head that night, he would have recognized that face anywhere. If he'd thought she was attractive in the moonlight, here in the glow of lanterns that hung on the walls and illuminated her features, she was strikingly beautiful.

His gaze did a slow study that started at the mass of braids that covered her head and ended at the polished toes of her feet. She was impeccably dressed in a blue blouse and a pair of black tailored slacks that gave her a cool sophisticated look. It was a look that was wreaking havoc on his male hormones. Even the anger he felt toward her couldn't diminish that fact, which was something that didn't sit too well with him at the moment. Nor did he appreciate the way his skin had tightened or the sudden feeling of raw, hungry desire that swept through his entire body.

Damn!

The last thing he needed was to be lusting after a woman whom he considered the enemy. But still, enemy or not, he couldn't stop the way his body responded when he watched her push her long braids back over her shoulders. And when she licked her lips with the tip of her tongue while glancing around, he thought he would literally go up in smoke. He definitely felt more than a slow burn coming on. It felt like someone had lit him with a blazing torch.

Heaven help him. A groan slipped past his throat the exact moment his senses took over, making him acutely aware of her. He tried to remember the last time he'd been with a woman, and then quickly decided it had been way too long. Several business deals had forced him to put his sex life on hold for a while, but seeing Jasmine Carmody made him remember just what he'd been missing.

He noted the exact moment her gaze found his and

watched her breathing change, becoming as irregular as his own. Something, he wasn't sure exactly what, hung in the air between them. Electrifying heat washed over him and he would swear she felt it, too, although a distance of about ten feet separated them. There were just some things that a man who'd been around as much as he had, knew. And the one thing that was clearly obvious was that he'd made a big mistake in asking her to meet him at the coffeehouse.

He should have confronted her where she worked. Once there, inside the walls of the newspaper office—a place he detested—he would not have cared if she were naked.

That was a lie and he knew it. He would have cared if she was naked—a lot.

She wavered before moving toward him and he hesitated before standing to make sure his knees wouldn't go weak on him. As usual, the coffeehouse was crowded and the last thing he wanted was to make a spectacle of himself. He tried to clear his head, but when the same luscious scent he now associated with Jasmine wafted into his nostrils, the idea was useless.

"Mr. Brooks," she said curtly, before taking a seat. She didn't offer him her hand, which was just as well since he probably would not have taken it anyway. They weren't friends and there was no need to pretend otherwise. Besides, he didn't want to touch her. Touching could lead to things he'd rather not think about.

"Ms. Carmody," he acknowledged, reclaiming his own seat. She was mad, he could tell. Evidently, she was used to having the upper hand, but tonight things would be different.

He watched her, saying nothing, as she skimmed her index finger across the tablecloth and met his gaze, showing him she wasn't easily intimidated. Her eyes were the color of chocolate chips, and staring into them was effortless.

When moments passed and neither of them made conversation, she finally said, "You indicated you had something of mine, Mr. Brooks."

The corner of Wesley's mouth curved into an amused smile when he heard the impatient edge in her tone. Did she actually think he would return her locket without first letting her know what he thought of her for invading his privacy? He didn't appreciate her using the Danforths as her ticket to fame. They were good people. He could attest to that. For the past fourteen years, they had been the only real family he'd ever known, and he didn't take kindly to anyone trying to dirty their good name.

He leaned back in his chair. "Yes, I did indicate that, didn't I? But first I want to know what you were doing going through my garbage that night."

Her tongue did a nervous sweep of her bottom lip and he wished she hadn't done that. He found himself shifting in his chair to relieve the pressure of a sudden ache in his lower body. And her scent wasn't helping matters. He would be in serious trouble if he didn't get a grip and push aside the sensual effects Jasmine Carmody was having on him.

"What makes you think I was going through your garbage?"

He lifted a brow at her question. Did she intend to play dumb? Then he would educate her quickly. "Because I saw you, Ms. Carmody. How would you like to be the one to make the front page for once? I can just see the headlines now and wonder what your boss at the *Savannah Morning News* would say if I told him what you did. There's a law against harassment and invasion of privacy, not to mention trespassing." From her expression he could tell that she didn't want to think what her boss would say, or the charges Wesley could possibly bring against her.

She sat up straight in her chair. "I was just doing my job."

He gave her a considering glance. "Since when did your job include breaking the law? If that's the case then maybe you should switch professions."

Jasmine breathed deeply, knowing he had a right to be upset and she would give him that right...to a point. "Look, I admit I went too far that night. I've never gone through anyone's garbage before. I was desperate."

Wesley narrowed his eyes at her. If she thought he would accept that as a good excuse then she had another thought coming. Caroline Perry had been desperate, too, and he had learned the hard way that desperate women, especially in her profession, couldn't be trusted. They didn't care who they hurt as long as they got their story.

"I'm glad you can easily admit to your desperation, Ms. Carmody, and I for one know that a desperate person will do just about anything. But I can't let you do that since you're so hell-bent on ruining the Danforths' good name. So I've decided to give you a taste of your own medicine. I want you to know how it feels to be followed and spied on every single day."

She contemplated him for a long moment, as if trying to figure out what he was saying. "What are you talking about?" she finally asked.

He smiled, but the smile didn't quite touch his eyes. "What I'm talking about is you not respecting the privacy of others. I will become your shadow."

He watched as she comprehended what he'd said. Her eyes widened then flashed with anger when she said. "You're going to stalk me?"

Wesley rolled his eyes upward. "Call it whatever you like, however, I think stalking is too strong a word. I see it merely as a way to keep you in line and out of trouble, especially until Abraham Danforth's senate race is over." It was easy to see that she was livid. Hellfire mad was a definite. Pretty damn pissed wasn't far behind.

"I have a job to do, Mr. Brooks," she stated in a clearly agitated voice like that was all the reason she needed.

Their gazes met, held, clashed for several seconds before he said, "Then do it, Ms. Carmody, but not at the expense of hurting innocent people. I know your kind. You're a reporter who will do anything for a story. I suggest you ask your boss to transfer you to the lifestyle section of the paper or the fashion column, something that suits you better."

"Now you look here—" she began, looking both hostile and beautiful at the same time.

"No, you look here," he said, his tone brittle. "I

will follow you around whether you like it or not. And if you complain to the police with some foolishness about me stalking you, then I will gladly file charges and have my attorney hit your newspaper with a gigantic lawsuit. And as far as your locket, I will keep it until I feel you deserve to have it back.''

''That's blackmail!''

Wesley smiled. ''I want to think of it as an investment of my time in your rehabilitation. It will be my guarantee that you'll leave the Danforths alone.''

She glared at him. ''That won't happen.''

''Then I'll continue to be your shadow and I'll keep your locket.''

She crossed her arms over her chest. ''You can't keep it. That locket belongs to me and I can prove it.''

''Prove anything you want, but you'll have a hard time explaining to a court of law how you lost it on my property.''

Angrily, Jasmine stood. ''As far as I'm concerned, this conversation is over.''

Wesley shrugged. ''Fine. You and I don't ever have to speak again, Ms. Carmody, just as long as you know I will be there watching your every move.''

She frowned. ''And I'm supposed to just accept that?''

He smiled at her. ''At the moment, you don't have a choice.''

Apparently she heard the deep finality in his voice and decided against further argument.

Without having anything else to say, she turned and walked out of the coffeehouse.

* * *

The man was a regular pain in the rear end, Jasmine thought, glancing in her rearview mirror. Wesley Brooks must have left the coffeehouse the minute she did in order for him to be following her. He was making sure she knew he intended to do just what he had said, starting tonight.

She couldn't really label him a stalker since she knew he didn't mean her any physical harm; emotional harm was another story. He just intended to drive her nuts by constantly being her shadow and watching her every move. She hoped that he wore out sooner than she did and she had no intentions of letting him get next to her. If he didn't have anything better to do with his time, then that was his problem.

She exhaled a deep breath when she recalled just how good he had looked at the coffeehouse. It had taken all of her resolve to focus on what he'd been saying and not on the movement of his mouth. He had the most sensuous pair of lips that she had ever seen on any man. They were full and appeared soft, although the words pouring from them had been harsh. Then there was his voice. She had heard the subtle warning in the deep, rich timbre, and for a brief moment she'd begun to think she was listening to and looking at a Morris Chestnut clone. But she had to grudgingly admit that not even her favorite Hollywood actor had the ability to fill her with unrequited lust like Wesley.

A sharp awareness had cut through her body the moment she had joined Wesley at the table. Her senses had been teased, stretched, ignited, and every time she had met his gaze, her breasts had tingled against the material of her blouse.

She shook her head and couldn't help but smile. She was definitely pathetic. Here the man was out to get her and all she could think about was…making love with him—which was unusual since she was still a virgin and damn proud of it. In fact, her stepsisters enjoyed calling her "Proud Mary."

Jasmine knew her stepsisters had been sexually active for a long time—probably since their high-school days. But she'd had more things to do with her time than to become a notch on some man's bedpost. Besides, she had decided that her education meant more to her than some jock with a high testosterone level. And while in college, she had been too busy making the grades to get serious about anyone.

She was only twenty-six and figured she had plenty of time to have sex. Until then, she intended to keep her clothes on and concentrate on trying to get as far ahead in her career as she could.

She made a turn at the next traffic light and sure enough, Wesley Brooks's silver-gray Mercedes sports car turned right along with her. She frowned wondering just how many cars the man owned. Today at lunch he had been driving a late model Corvette. But then, when you had money you could do just about anything.

Moments later she pulled into her apartment complex and wasn't surprised when he pulled in right behind her. She parked her car and released her seat belt to get out. He parked next to her and was already out of his vehicle. He leaned against it and glared at her.

"You, Ms. Carmody, are a speeder."

She narrowed her eyes at him. "And you, Mr. Brooks, are a nuisance."

He shrugged. "I've been called worse."

She could just imagine some of the names he had been called. Deciding not to say anything else to him, she turned and walked toward her apartment. Unlocking her door, she glanced over her shoulder to take one last look at him. He was still leaning against his car glaring at her.

Without saying anything else to him, she quickly opened the door and went inside.

Wesley watched her close the door behind her and frowned. He experienced a moment of regret that he wasn't going inside her apartment with her. He didn't like the direction his thoughts were taking. He sighed, deciding that he would return to the coffeehouse and hang out there until it was time to show up at Ian's place to play cards.

Less than ten minutes later, he was parking his car back at the coffeehouse. The original coffeehouse was located in the historical district of Savannah and was a popular hangout with the young professional crowd and some older coffee lovers, as well. The coffeehouse made every kind of coffee imaginable and even had their own specialty blend, which was a real hit with customers, including him.

One of the most popular features of the coffeehouse was the bulletin board that was set up near the front of the shop. The board had taken on a life of its own and there was always a crowd of people surrounding it. Messages being sent back and forth by customers, particularly single customers, were taped on the board and Wesley had heard that several romances had been sparked because of the board.

He glanced around when he walked in. The coffee-house was a real cozy affair but there hadn't been anything cozy about his meeting tonight with Jasmine Carmody. Even when backed against a wall the woman had come out scratching, which a part of him couldn't help but admire. A frown creased his brow. He didn't want to admire anything about Jasmine Carmody. He had only to think for a second to remember how he had walked up on her going through his trash, and how he had offered her five hundred dollars of his hard earned cash because he actually thought she was someone who needed it.

He found a table near the back and a waitress quickly came to take his order. After being served, he leaned back in his chair as a scowl touched his face. The woman was destined to drive him nuts.

"You okay, Wes?"

Wesley looked up and found his good friend Reid Danforth standing next to his table with a concerned look on his face. Reid was Abraham's second oldest son and the director of Danforth and Company's shipping operation.

"Yes, I'm fine," he replied as Reid slipped into the chair across from him. "Any word yet on the body that was found at Crofthaven?"

In the course of renovation on Crofthaven, Abraham Danforth's mansion, the body of a young woman had been found in the attic. The ensuing police investigation had threatened to engulf Abraham Danforth's senate campaign in a scandal before it could get off the ground. Everyone was wondering who the woman was. When dental records proved the body was not that of Victoria Danforth, Jake's sister who had vanished without a trace after attending a concert nearly five years ago. Speculation remained as to who was involved in her disappearance. Like everyone else, he had fond memories of Tori and thanked God it wasn't her body that had been found.

"No, I haven't heard anything yet," Reid said, and at that moment the waitress came to take Reid's coffee order.

Wesley took a sip of his coffee, then asked, "How's Tina?" Reid was engaged to marry a beautiful young woman by the name of Tina Morgan and Wes was happy for his good friend.

Reid smiled. "Tina is fine and I'm glad she came into my life. I can't wait until the day we get married."

Wesley nodded thinking that Reid and Jake had hit gold in finding women like Tina and Larissa, but as far as he was concerned, as long as there were women out there like Jasmine Carmody, he was determined to stay single.

Jasmine was in the bed when her phone rang less than an hour later. Glancing at her caller-ID box, she picked it up. "So, you finally decided to call to make sure I was still alive," she said to Ronnie. During her drive to the coffeehouse, she had used her cell phone to call Ronnie to tell her about Wesley Brooks's phone call and her plans to meet him.

"Well, what did he say?" Ronnie asked eagerly.

It took Jasmine less than ten minutes to tell Ronnie everything that had transpired.

"And he actually plans to follow you around?" Ronnie asked, clearly astonished.

"That's what he says and I have no reason not to believe him since he followed me home tonight. It wouldn't surprise me if he's parked outside when I leave for work in the morning since he's hell-bent on teaching me a lesson."

Ronnie chuckled. "Considering how he feels about reporters, it doesn't surprise me."

Jasmine lifted a brow. "And just how does he feel about reporters? I got the distinct impression that we aren't exactly his favorite people. Is there a story I should know about?" she asked, curiously. She knew that Ronnie's brother, Richard, had attended the same college as Wesley and Jacob Danforth at about the same time.

"Your family have only been living in Savannah for around eight years, Jazz. I think it's pretty common knowledge to those of us who've lived here most of our lives that Wesley dated some girl when he went off to Georgia Tech who was a journalism student. I even heard he had fallen hard for her, but that she had only been using him to write some article for the school paper. It was an article that got him kicked off the football team."

"Wow," Jasmine said, thinking that getting kicked off a college football team was pretty serious stuff. "But, still, that's no reason to take things out on me since I'm a reporter."

"Yeah, but you did go on his property and rummage through his trash cans."

Jasmine lifted a dark brow. "Hey, whose side are you on?"

Ronnie laughed. "Yours, of course, since I'm also a reporter and I've done some pretty crazy things, too. But personally, I think you're getting obsessed with this Danforth thing, to the point where you'll do just about anything to break a story."

Jasmine frowned. "Ronnie, that's not fair. You sound like you think I don't have any ethics."

"And I'm sorry if I sound that way, but think about it, Jazz. Ever since you were assigned to cover Abraham Danforth's campaign, you've been determined to dig up anything and everything on him that you can."

Jasmine shrugged. "I just want to report the truth."

"Yes, but why are you so convinced there is something he's hiding?"

Jasmine frowned deepened. "And why are you convinced there isn't?"

Ronnie chuckled. "Like I said earlier, I grew up in this town. The Danforths have been around forever. That doesn't make them saints but I personally think of them as good people. And as far as Abraham Danforth is concerned, he's pretty well liked which is why he has a lot of supporters. So be careful, a lot of people won't like you trying to sully his name."

All she had to do was think of Wesley Brooks to know that was true. Before Jasmine finally drifted off to sleep an hour or so later, she couldn't help but think about the conversation she'd had with Ronnie. Had she become so obsessed with breaking a story that she had started being unfair and biased?

She swallowed hard when she thought about just how pushy she'd been with Larissa Neilson in trying to get the woman to admit that Jacob Danforth had fathered her child.

She tossed and turned, trying to find a comfortable position in bed, determined to put Wesley Brooks, as well as the Danforths, out of her mind. A few minutes later she discovered it was easy putting the Danforths out of her thoughts, but getting rid of Wesley Brooks was a little more challenging.

Even when Jasmine finally drifted off to sleep, she couldn't keep Wesley from creeping into her dreams.

Three

———

The next morning, while sitting at her kitchen table drinking a cup of coffee, Jasmine pulled out a folder to review all the information she had gathered on Abraham Danforth so far.

One thing she'd discovered about the man was that he was an overachiever. He'd been the first son born to the prominent Savannah Danforths, and as such he'd been expected to be the best at everything. Entering the military he rose to the rank of Navy SEAL commander. He married Chloe Forsythe, who represented the crème de la crème of Savannah society and she bore him five children. Jasmine's report also indicated that while serving in Vietnam on a dangerous mission, Abraham had gotten injured.

When Abraham's wife died, he was at the height of his military career and knew he couldn't provide the kind of nurturing presence his children needed. He'd arranged for his children to attend the finest boarding schools and had asked his younger brother Harold to step in on the holidays when he was gone.

Jasmine pulled out a color photograph of Abraham Danforth and had to admit he was very good-looking for his age. His hair was a dark brown and his eyes were a beautiful color of blue. At fifty-six, he had an athletic physique which was probably due to all the hours he spent at a health club. Single and wealthy, he would be a prize catch for any woman. She couldn't help wondering why he had never remarried or why his name wasn't romantically linked to anyone. Maybe that was something she needed to look at more closely.

Jasmine sighed deeply as she pushed her notes on Abraham Danforth aside. The man who'd once had a distinguished military career now wanted to be a senator. There had to be something in his background that was worth checking out and uncovering. No one could have such an unsullied past.

And what about the rumor that threatening e-mails had been sent to him? As well as the question as to who was responsible for crashing his computer with a virus and why? Both incidents sounded like the man had an enemy that she needed to know about.

She glanced at her watch. It was time she got dressed and went in to work. She intended to drop by the library some time today and research information about the women in Abraham Danforth's life. More specifically, the names of the women he had dated within the past twenty-four months. There was a possibility that one of them had something interesting to tell.

An hour or so later after arriving at work, she was sent to city hall to cover the mayor's press conference where he announced the city's proposed budget cuts. After the press conference ended, like the other reporters that were present, she began jotting down last-minute quotes on her laptop.

Jasmine shivered when she felt someone's hot breath stir against her neck. She turned around quickly, only to collide with Wesley Brooks.

She took a step away from him and released an exasperated sigh, determined to be cool and not let him know he was ruining her normally good attitude. Because she'd dreamed of him all through the night, she had awoken edgy and irritated.

"Interested in politics, Mr. Brooks?" she asked curtly. The one thing she immediately noted was the fact that he seemed taller to her today. Taller, more overwhelming and just as sexy.

He crossed his arms over his chest and stared at her. "No, but I am interested in you. I hope you've been staying out of trouble."

She narrowed her eyes and lifted her chin, and encountered the same ruthless glint in his gaze that had been there the night before. "My job is to report the news. That's what I'm doing and what I've always done."

"Oh? And that includes going through someone's trash?"

Jasmine lifted her gaze up to the ceiling. "You have social status in this community, Mr. Brooks. Surely someone has invaded your privacy before. Do you want me to believe you've never been hounded by the paparazzi? What about that time last year when it was rumored that you were seeing that well-known professional model?''

He shrugged. ''That was different.''

She lifted a dark brow. ''In what way?''

''It was different because I decided to tolerate it then, and because it was about me. You going through my garbage wasn't about me. It was about your efforts to start a smear campaign against someone I care deeply about and respect. But I guess you probably don't know much about care and respect.''

She was taken aback by his assumption. ''For your information I care for and respect my father deeply.''

''Your father?''

She couldn't help but smile. ''Yes, my father. Didn't you think I had one?''

He glared. ''When it comes to you, I really didn't know what to think. When I first saw you, I thought you were a homeless person.''

She nodded, remembering how he had offered her money and food. She felt bad about that. She snapped her laptop shut and began walking. He automatically began walking beside her. ''Well,'' she said, trying to ignore him, ''as you can see I am not homeless.''

He raked his gaze over her. ''Yeah, tell me about it.''

She stopped walking and glanced up at him and said, ''Look, I'm really sorry about that.''

He looked into her eyes. ''Are you?''

She felt the need to clarify. ''Not for going through

your garbage but for you thinking I needed a handout. It was kind of you to offer me money and food.''

"I'm usually a kind person,'' he said in a low voice right beside her.

Until he feels someone is trying to use him or is hurting someone he cares about, she thought as she began walking again. He walked silently beside her until they reached her car. She noticed he had parked next to her. He turned and looked at her. "So where to now, Ms. Carmody?''

She shook her head. "Don't you think you're taking this a little too far?''

"No further than you took things when you went through my trash,'' he said leaning against his car.

She was about to say something but at that particular moment her mobile phone rang. "Yes?''

Her eyes widened. "When?''

She then sighed deeply. "All right. Thanks for letting me know.'' She slipped her mobile phone back into her purse and looked at him. "I just heard something that might interest you, Mr. Brooks.''

He lifted a brow. "What?''

"That was my boss. A definite identification has been made on the body that was found in the attic at Crofthaven.''

Wesley straightened. "Who was it?'' he inquired quietly.

Jasmine cleared her throat. She knew how much this information meant to him. "The body was identified as Martha Jones.''

Wesley inhaled deeply. Martha Jones had been the troubled and sickly daughter of Joyce Jones, the Danforths' long-time housekeeper. His heart went out to Joyce.

He met Jasmine's gaze. "And I bet you're determined to find Joyce Jones to get the scoop."

She frowned. "Yes, I'd definitely like to talk to her."

Wesley narrowed his gaze at her. "Don't you ever let up? The last thing Joyce needs right now is a nosey newspaper reporter asking her questions. She probably needs this time alone."

Jasmine scowled. "I'm not an insensitive person."

He glared. "Really? You had me fooled. Only an insensitive person would have hassled Larissa about the identify of her baby's father."

She placed her hands on her hips. "It's my job to report any news-breaking stories. And I considered that news breaking. Anything that goes on in the Danforths' household is newsworthy. Now if you'll excuse me, I have a job to do."

Wesley sighed. The woman was wearing on his last nerve and he forced himself to stay calm in the wake of his rising anger. He moved aside when she got into her car. He had meant what he said, he intended to be her shadow and somehow he would get through it. She would be a challenge but he'd overcome challenges before. Jasmine Carmody was nothing compared to others he'd faced. As a kid, being carted from one foster home to another had been a challenge, as well as a pain…literally.

He had to keep his head on straight and remember that she was just a woman and he'd known plenty. But then there was something that made her stand out, something distinctively different. As he got into his car to follow her to her next destination—which he knew would be Crofthaven—the only thing he could think about was that a woman like Jasmine could mess with a man's mind.

His mind he could control. He hoped and prayed he could control the rest of his body.

Although she wanted to appear cool on the outside, Jasmine was in turmoil on the inside. The more she thought about Wesley Brooks, the angrier she became. And she didn't understand how she could be attracted to a man like him. It was disgusting.

By the time she arrived at Crofthaven, several television news crews were there to set up for a press conference. The huge estate on the outskirts of Savannah housed a large Georgian-style mansion. The house was considered a historical landmark as it was built over one hundred years ago. The grounds surrounding Crofthaven were lush and lovely, and no doubt tended by a whole army of gardeners, Jasmine thought. Magnificent moss-covered oak trees lined the drive to the main house. The land stretched all the way to the Atlantic and Jasmine picked up the potent scent of the ocean.

She quickly parked her car and got out, determined to find out as much information as she could. She glanced around and saw another reporter from the *Savannah Morning News* and waved. Brad Cabot answered her greeting with a full-fledge boyish grin. Fresh out of college, he had only been working for the paper a year and she had found him to be good company during the times they had gone out on assignments together.

"What's going on?" she asked the minute he walked up.

"Not much. The family plans to make a statement in a few minutes so you got here just in time."

Jasmine nodded at the same time she glanced around and saw Wesley's car pull up. Her eyes narrowed and a frown touched her lips as she watched him get out of his car. Reporters rushed over to him, wanting a statement, a comment, just about any information he could provide. Without responding to the vast number of questions being thrown at him, he steadily moved up the steps of the huge mansion toward the front door.

Jasmine watched him, and as if he felt the heat of her gaze, he turned and looked at her. Her eyes immediately went to the strong lines of his face, especially the darkness of his eyes, the fullness of his lips and the firmness of his chin. She drew in a quick, shaky breath and her heart thumped crazily in her chest as their gazes met and held. He frowned and she felt his disapproval all the way to her toes.

She also felt something else. Cutting through all of his anger she felt an intense attraction. She swallowed when his gaze continued to stay welded to hers, unable to move. Then moments later he turned before opening the door and entering Crofthaven.

"I take it that the two of you know each other," Brad said grinning, glancing over his shoulder at her. It had been clearly obvious that Wesley's gaze had singled her out.

She shrugged and replied in a carefully neutral tone. "Yes, we've run into each other a few times."

"And what do you think of him?"

Jasmine didn't want to think of him at all. She met Brad's gaze. "I think he's...interesting."

A few hours later and Jasmine was pretty sure Wesley Brooks was more than interesting. He was beginning to become a nuisance. Even now while she did her grocery shopping, she knew that he was somewhere watching her.

At the press conference at Crofthaven, Abraham Danforth had spoken on behalf of the Danforth family and acknowledged that the body found in the attic had been that of his long-time housekeeper's daughter. He'd further stated that the hearts of the Danforths went out to the Jones's family.

In Jasmine's opinion, Abraham Danforth had handled the media like a true politician and had only perfected his squeaky clean image. He assured everyone that he was one hundred percent behind the investigation to determine the cause of Martha's death and he wanted to find out the truth as much as anyone. While he had been talking she was aware that Wesley, standing united with the members of the Danforth family, had been watching her.

Like he was still doing.

She glanced around the supermarket. Although she didn't see him anywhere, she felt his presence.

"Did you find everything you needed?" the woman asked her at checkout.

"Yes, thanks," she replied. She then glanced over

her shoulder to see Wesley Brooks coming up to stand directly behind her with a ton of microwave spaghetti dinners in his hand.

"Stocking up on dinner, Mr. Brooks?" she asked after accepting her change back from the cashier.

"No more than you're stocking up on junk food," he countered, looking at her purchases that consisted of a pair of panty hose, a celebrity magazine, several bars of Snickers and a pint-size carton of chocolate chip cookie dough ice cream.

"This is energy food," she said, deciding she didn't like him seeing what she had bought.

"And this is energy food, as well." He then glanced at his watch. "I hope you're calling it a day and are on your way home."

She lifted a brow. "And if I'm not?"

"Then I'll have to follow you around some more."

She wanted to tell him to stop following her and get a life. But the last thing she needed to do was make him angry; she'd never get her locket back that way.

Jasmine had decided last night while in bed that the best way to deal with Wesley Brooks was to ignore him—which wasn't an easy thing to do.

"Don't try keeping up with me," she said, tossing the words over her shoulder as she accepted the grocery bag the cashier handed her.

"Oh, but I will keep up with you and I must say I found your activities today rather interesting."

"Don't you have a company to run?" she asked angrily.

"Yes, and being my own boss gives me the flexibility to make my own hours and I've decided to work them around your schedule.''

"How accommodating," she snapped.

He smiled. "Yes, I think so."

Jasmine frowned. This was the first time she had seen him since she'd left the press conference at Crofthaven. Martha Jones and Victoria Danforth had become missing within two years of each other, and Jasmine had left the press conference feeling rather suspicious of that fact. She couldn't help wondering if Wesley was letting her know that he'd been hot on her tail when she'd left the press conference for the library to research old newspaper articles regarding the disappearances of both women. While she was at the library she had also decided to check into information on Abraham Danforth's social life and the women involved in it.

Deciding not to engage in conversation with Wesley Brooks any longer, she gripped the bag firmly in her hand and walked out the door into the well-lit parking lot. When she got to her car she noted he was parked next to her. She pretended not to pay any attention when he went to his own car. He glanced over at her.

"You didn't ask as many questions as I expected at today's press conference," he said putting his grocery bag in the back seat of his car. "I was impressed."

She glared at him. "Don't be. There will be other days, trust me."

Wesley held her glare, emitting one of his own. "But I don't trust you. Ms. Carmody, and doubt that I ever will." He opened his car door to get in. "I suggest you go on home before your ice cream melts."

Without waiting for her to respond he slipped inside his car and started the engine. But he didn't move his vehicle until she had angrily gotten into hers and pulled out.

Glancing into her rearview mirror Jasmine saw that he was determined to follow her to her door. She inhaled deeply, thinking it would be a waste of energy to lose her temper. If the man had nothing else to do then that was his business and she refused to let him get to her.

But a part of her knew it was too late. He had already gotten to her and it would be a sheer act of will on her part to ignore him.

Wesley smiled when he pulled into his driveway to find Imogene Danforth sitting in her car and waiting on him. He was pleased, as well as surprised, to see her since they hadn't got the chance to talk much at the press conference earlier that day. Everyone knew that Imogene was one very busy woman, almost working obsessively as an investment banker to move up the corporate ladder. She was known to eat on the run while conducting business over the phone.

He also knew that Imogene put a lot of stock in her appearance. She always chose just the right clothes, the right haircut and the right possessions. She saw all those things as essential in succeeding in the cutthroat business world of finance.

After he parked his car and got out, he watched Jake's little sister get out of the sporty Lexus. He leaned against his car and frowned as he stared at the very attractive woman who was walking toward him dressed in an expensive navy-blue powerhouse business suit with matching shoes. She had her briefcase in one hand, a candy bar in the other, munching in between the conversation she was having on the cell phone headset that was plugged into her ear.

By the time she had reached him, whatever conversation she'd been holding had ended and she'd pulled off the headset, snapped the phone shut and slipped it into her purse at the same time she swallowed the last of the candy bar.

"Wes, I'm glad you finally came home. I thought I would die of starvation."

Wesley lifted a brow. "You must really be hungry to confess that you are, Imogene. I thought you promised your parents that you would improve your eating habits."

The attractive blond-haired, green-eyed woman standing in front of him lifted a brow of her own. "I'll start eating better when you do." She glanced at the grocery bag he held in his hand. "So, what's for dinner?"

Wesley shook his head grinning. "Spaghetti."

She smiled. "That figures, and I hope there's one to spare. I have another appointment in about an hour."

A half hour later Imogene was finishing off the last of her microwave spaghetti dinner with a glass of white wine. She smiled over at the man she considered one of her brothers. "Maybe you need to rethink my offer of investing in this food company since you seem to enjoy their product so much."

Wes smiled as he leaned back in his chair. "We've

had this conversation before, Imogene, and the answer is still no."

She returned his smile. "I was hoping you would have changed your mind."

"Not hardly, so go harass another client."

Imogene giggled as she leaned back in her own chair. "So what's going on with you, Wes, other than not eating properly? It seems Mom has the both of us on her 'worry about' list. She called this morning and asked that I check up on you to make sure you were eating properly."

Wesley shook his head. "Umm, that's interesting. When I saw her at Crofthaven today, she mentioned something to me about checking up on you, as well."

Imogene frowned. "That figures." After a few moments she said. "But what doesn't figure is the looks you were giving that reporter at the press conference. Is there something I should know, Wes?"

Wesley raised a dark brow. Imogene had been on the phone the majority of the time trying to cut deals. He was surprised that she had noticed him looking at Jasmine Carmody.

"Isn't she that same reporter who's been snooping around trying to dig up stuff on the family?" Imogene went on to ask when he didn't answer her earlier question.

After taking a sip of his own wine, Wesley answered. "Yes, she's the same one. And my interest in her is purely business. I'm keeping an eye on her."

Imogene smiled over the rim of her wineglass. "Well, that much was obvious. How is keeping an eye on her business?"

"Because I'm making it my business to see that she stops harassing the family."

Imogene nodded. "That should be interesting and I'd love to hear the full details later." She glanced at her watch and stood. "Time's up. I've got to run. Thanks for dinner."

Wesley stood and he opened his mouth to tell her she needed to slow down and take care of herself more, but he knew he would be wasting his time. "You know you're welcome anytime."

He walked her to the door and watched as she got into her car and sped off. After checking his watch, he decided to tackle the work he had brought home with him.

A few hours later, Wesley shut down his computer when he reached a mental block, a first for him. Standing, he stretched and moved away from his desk and walked over to the window.

He loved his new home, especially the view he had of the Savannah River from his office, his bedroom and several other rooms in the house. As a kid, the river had always given him peace and whenever he ran away from one of his foster homes, the area surrounding the river would be the first place he would go to hide.

But this evening the river didn't deliver the peace and tranquility it normally did and all because of Jasmine Carmody. Earlier today he hadn't been able to concentrate on what Abraham had been saying at the press conference because he'd been distracted by her. If Imogene had noticed, he wondered if the rest of the family had, too.

It seemed that his gaze had automatically located Jasmine in the crowd and had latched on to the mass of braids on her head, her sexy body and her cool and confident posture. The funny thing was that women constantly threw themselves at him, yet his thoughts had never been filled with any of them like they were with Jasmine. But here was a woman who loathed him and didn't want to give him the time of day and his mind was filled with nothing but her.

He turned when he heard the phone ring and walked back to his desk to answer it. "Yes?"

"Wes, it's Ian."

Wesley smiled. "Ian, what's going on? If you're calling to gloat about winning the poker game last night, forget it because—"

"She's here," Ian interrupted by saying. "At the coffeehouse."

Wesley raised a brow as he sat down. "Who's at the coffeehouse?"

"The woman you told us about last night. The one you caught going through your garbage. That reporter, Jasmine Carmody."

A frown covered Wesley's face and he sat up straight in his chair. When he had seen her earlier at the grocery store, she had led him to believe that she was heading home and would be in for the rest of the night. In fact one of the main reasons he hadn't been able to concentrate while working on his computer was because of the visions he'd had of Jasmine sitting cross-legged in the middle of her bed, wearing very little, while eating her carton of ice cream, and thumbing through the magazine she had purchased earlier.

In his mind he saw her legs and appreciated just how long and shapely they were.

"How do you know it's her when you've never seen her before?" he asked Ian.

"Because Jake was here when she came in and he pointed her out to me. He said she's the one who'd been sniffing around trying to dig up something on the family. Then I remembered what you told us, so I've been keeping my eye on her and she's here tonight sniffing. One of the waitresses said she's been asking questions about Dad."

Damn. Wesley squeezed his eyes shut and silently counted to ten. He reopened them as he stood and said. "I'm on my way."

Four

Jasmine sat forward and rested her forearms on the table as she glanced around the coffeehouse. She was getting bored.

She'd already been here for an hour and so far she hadn't found out anything about Abraham Danforth that she hadn't already known. The waitress who had waited on her hadn't been too chatty and when she had spoken, it was to sing Abraham Danforth's praises. It seemed that everyone wanted to share the good stuff about him but no one was willing to divulge the bad.

She glanced across the room and knew the man looking at her so intently was Ian Danforth, Abraham's oldest son and CEO of Danforth and Company. She heard he frequented the coffee shop since he, along with his brother Adam and cousin Jacob were the owners. She'd also heard that he was a playboy which wouldn't surprise her, given what she'd been able to dig up on the very handsome man with wavy brown hair and hazel eyes.

A Duke University graduate, he had married at twenty-two because his girlfriend had gotten pregnant. A few months into the marriage, the woman had lost the baby. Somehow it had been revealed that she'd never wanted Ian or the baby, just Ian's money. Subsequently the marriage ended in a divorce. Over the years, his sister and cousins had tried playing matchmaker but from what Jasmine gathered, Ian Danforth only dated women that he was in no danger of falling in love with.

Jasmine had even gone so far as to do research to locate his ex-wife, Lara, to see if there was any scoop the woman had wanted to share but hadn't been able to find her. After leaving Savannah, Lara Danforth appeared to have fallen off the face of the earth.

Jasmine decided to shift her thoughts to something else—something pleasant. She thought about the interview she had done last week. The article had appeared in today's paper and her editor had been very generous with his praise. The interview had been with a female teacher who had recently returned from Iraq and had shared her year-long experience. It was too bad that stories like those couldn't advance a reporter's career to the next level. The majority of the reading public wanted to know about a famous person's sordid past and juicy present, especially if that person was a "wanna be" politician like Abraham

Danforth. Those were the type of stories that could boost a reporter's career.

Jasmine took a sip of her coffee thinking how good it tasted. There were several D&D coffeehouses around the city and she usually dropped into one from time to time to drink coffee and eat a danish or two.

She glanced around, wondering whom she could possibly make conversation with that might have the information she needed. She'd heard that of all the coffeehouses, this was the one Abraham Danforth frequented the most. It was also rumored that he usually made an appearance with his PR person, Nicola Granville, every Wednesday night to discuss strategy over coffee. Jasmine hoped that if that meeting took place tonight, she would be within listening range. There was no telling the information she could pick up from that discussion.

Suddenly, Jasmine felt a warmth slide up her spine and she shifted her gaze to the entrance of the coffeehouse.

Wesley Brooks.

Their gazes connected and she inhaled slowly. The man was frowning. Her hand tightened around the cup of coffee she held in her hand, bracing herself for the anger she felt radiating from him all the way across the room. She had never known a man who could look so good when he was mad. And, boy, did he look good. *Marvelous* was a better word. She would even go so far to use the word *striking*.

Wearing a pair of jeans that looked like they were custom-made for his body, and a pullover shirt, he looked delicious, good enough to eat or to lick all over. She blinked, not believing the direction of her thoughts but lately she'd found that Wesley Brooks had featured prominently in her sexual fantasies; fantasies she'd never had until meeting him.

She let out a long, deep sigh. So what if she found him attractive. She was a woman and he was a man. No big deal. But as she continued to hold his angry gaze, she decided it was a *big* deal when they each considered the other the enemy. He was determined to put himself in the path of what she wanted, what she needed the most—a news-breaking story.

As he slowly skirted around several tables to head her way, she vowed not to be intimidated by him. She lifted her chin, refusing to turn to mush as the strong, well-defined muscles of his chest and shoulders became more defined by the glow of lanterns burning on the walls. His jeans and the way he was wearing them made every woman in the place sensually aware of him as a man. She didn't miss the number of female heads that turned to look at him.

Mercy, she thought. The man was filling her vision. He was also filling something else; a desire to release the suppressed hormones trying to spring to life inside of her. She'd always thought of herself as a good girl but tonight, this very second, the thoughts flooding her mind weren't good. They were racy, torrid…just plain bad.

Jasmine self-consciously cleared her throat when he came nearer, and tried to ignore the way her body was reacting. Her blouse suddenly felt too tight against her breasts. She frowned, not liking the thought that Wesley Brooks could fill her with hot sensations whenever he was within a hundred feet of her. But then from the articles she had read in the paper in the society columns, women drooled over him all the time, which was one of the reasons he had a reputation for being an irresistible ladies' man. Now that Jake Danforth was married off, Wesley Brooks's and Ian Danforth's names headed Savannah's list as the city's most eligible bachelors; bachelors that any woman would want.

When he came to a stop at her table, she leaned back in her chair and exhaled a long, deep breath. He was upset at seeing her here tonight. It then dawned on her that he was upset but not surprised. In fact, he had walked in like he had expected to find her, which meant someone had tipped him off. She glanced over at Ian Danforth and he gave her a mega-watt smile. She frowned. The man had obviously snitched on her.

She shrugged. This was a free country and she had the right to go wherever she wanted. If Wesley thought just because he was holding her locket hostage that he could dictate how she spent her evenings, then he had another thought coming. Thanks to her stepmother and stepsisters, she had learned a long time ago how to stick up for herself and not let anyone run her life. She might have little control over Wesley Brooks dominating her dreams but she refused to let him command the hours while she was awake.

So as calmly as she could, she returned his stare as she gripped the coffee cup tighter in her hand. She twisted her lips in a forced smile. "Wesley, funny seeing you here."

* * *

There was nothing funny about it at all, Wesley thought, meeting her gaze. Whenever he saw her, his hormones shifted into overdrive and visions of naked bodies, silken sheets and thrusting motions danced in his head.

Jasmine Carmody just might be the death of him; but before he died, he wanted to do something outrageous like reach across the table, snatch her up in his arms and mold her smart-ass mouth against his.

Without waiting for an invitation he knew he'd never get, he took the chair across from her. "What are you doing here, Jasmine?"

She smiled at him. Again. "What does it look like I'm doing? I'm sitting here minding my own business, drinking a cup of coffee and eating a danish. Is that a crime?"

Wesley shrugged. "Not if you were really minding your own business. But it's my understanding that you've been asking questions."

She sighed. Evidently the waitress had talked. There would be no tip for her tonight. "Asking questions is part of my job."

"Then consider yourself officially off work."

Jasmine's gaze narrowed. "I'm never off work."

Wesley replaced the frown with a slow smile, but it was a smile that didn't quite reach his eyes. "Then I guess I'll have to change that."

He stood and pulled several bills out of the pocket of his jeans and tossed them on the table. "Come on."

She blinked. "Excuse me?"

He leaned forward, bracing his hands on the table.

"I said come on. It's time you stop working and have fun and I know just the place to take you."

To the gallows to chop off her head no doubt, Jasmine thought as she eyed him warily. She was curious and intrigued, but not stupid. And although she had no intentions of going anywhere with him, she asked anyway. "Where?"

"To the country fair that's in town."

Jasmine leaned back in her chair. The fair came to town every year and she couldn't recall the last time she had gone. Suddenly her mouth watered at the thought of a candied apple, cotton candy and popcorn, not to mention the rides. She wondered what she had to lose if she decided to indulge in a little fun. It then occurred to her that she could possibly lose out on getting the scoop on Abraham Danforth if he showed up here tonight. But then she doubted Wesley would let her follow through with any plan she'd made concerning Abraham tonight anyway. Besides, after the short conversation she'd had with her stepmother earlier, she needed to do something that would make her scream, and a roller-coaster ride just might do the trick.

However, there was another stumbling block. If she went with Wesley to the fair, some people might construe it as a date.

She crossed her arms over her chest knowing he had an ulterior motive for asking her to the fair. Was something going down tonight that she needed to know about? "Why?"

He lifted a brow. "Why what?"

"Why do you want to take me to the fair?"

He smiled. "I just told you. I think you work too much. You need to have fun, live a little, let your hair down and play," he said, reaching out and pulling on one of her braids.

He may as well have been pulling on the nipples of her breasts from the sensation that suddenly zipped to their sensitive tips. It had sent a jolt right through her. Unfortunately, her body's reaction only proved she had a lot of nervous energy to work off so maybe going to the fair was not a bad idea.

"And there's no reason for you not to go, unless…"

She lifted a brow. "Unless what?"

"Unless you don't think you can handle me."

Jasmine frowned. Truthfully, she doubted she could handle him, but she would never let him know that. She had learned the hard way to never let anyone know her weaknesses. "You're nothing to handle, Wesley," she lied, meeting his gaze.

His smile widened and he leaned closer and whispered, "Prove it."

She blinked wondering how such a thing could be proven. Evidently he was used to women seducing him. To him this was all a game, a game that he knew the rules to and was well versed at playing.

Jasmine sighed, not able to think straight with such a gorgeous set of hazel eyes staring at her. She wondered if she would regret her decision in the morning.

"All right," she said standing. "Just for tonight, we'll call a truce and have some fun. But tomorrow it's back to work as usual."

Wesley chuckled and decided not to tell her that

once she began playing with him, work would never be the same again.

Moments later they were walking out of the coffee-house. "We'll go in my car and I'll bring you back here afterward to get yours," Wesley said, as they stepped into the parking lot.

Jasmine nodded as he led her toward his car. Tonight he was driving the Corvette again.

He unlocked the passenger car door for her and she slipped into the smooth leather seat. She immediately tugged her skirt down when she noted his gaze drifted to her exposed thighs and legs.

"Thanks and you can close the door now," she said, when he continued to stand there.

"All right," he said, meeting her gaze once more before closing the door. He rounded the hood and opened the driver's door to get in. "So how long have you lived in Savannah?"

She glanced over at him. "For eight years, ever since college. I came here to attend Savannah State and my father decided to accept a position at the hospital to be near me."

Wesley nodded. "Dr. James Carmody, head of orthopedics?" When he'd first found out her name, he had wondered if she was related to the doctor. Carmody wasn't a common name in these parts.

She raised a brow. "Yes, you know him?"

"We've met," Wesley said, backing up the car and heading toward the expressway. "We've run into each other at several social functions." He glanced over at her. "I've also met your mother and your sisters before but I never knew the doctor had a third daughter."

Jasmine turned and met his gaze when she again remembered the conversation she'd had with her stepmother earlier. "You met my *stepmother* and *stepsisters*. Biologically, I'm my father's only child and although he's never legally adopted my stepsisters, they find it very convenient to use my father's last name."

Wesley nodded and remembered the woman in the locket was not the woman he'd met who'd tried throwing her two daughters at him. Evidently there was no love lost between Jasmine, her stepmother and stepsisters, Wesley thought, as he kept his gaze on the road. He decided to file that information away just in case he needed to use it later.

"So where are you from originally?" he decided to ask her.

"I was born in Louisiana and lived there until my mother died when I was nine. The memories of my mother's death were too much for my father, so he transferred to a hospital in L.A. It was there that he met my stepmother and they married when I turned sixteen."

Jasmine didn't ask him about his background since she'd heard the story already. Although he hadn't had a family to call his own in the past, he definitely had one now with the Danforths. They claimed him as part of their family and according to Ronnie, the Danforths were very protective of him…just as much as he was of them.

The conversation between them came to an end. In a way she preferred the silence and took a moment to appreciate the night. There were stars in the sky and a full moon overhead and since they were close to the

Atlantic coast, she could smell the ocean, and with the window down she could pick up the scent of the wild-flowers in bloom. Spring was her most favorite time of the year.

It was a beautiful night, and a part of her was grateful to Wesley for taking her away…even if he had an ulterior motive in doing so. She smiled. Tonight he intended to pick her brain instead of letting her pick someone else's.

"The fair doesn't look crowded," Wesley said, breaking into Jasmine's thoughts when they had reached the fair grounds.

As he pulled into a parking space she immediately picked up the scent of hot dogs, cooked onions and popcorn. "Probably because tomorrow is a school day. They must get most of their business on the week-ends."

Wesley grinned. "That's good since it means no long lines." He turned off the car's ignition and turned to her. "Come on, let's have fun."

Four hours later an exhausted Jasmine felt tired and drained as they made it back to Wesley's car. She had never realized that having fun could sap a person of all their energy.

"Are you sure it will be all right for my car to stay at the coffeehouse all night? I'd hate to return in the morning to find it's been towed away," she was barely able to get out the words she felt so worn out. All she could do was slip into the car when he opened the door. Moments later when she heard the sound of the ignition, she decided to relax with her head back against the headrest and closed her eyes. There was no way she could drive home tonight and appreciated Wesley for offering to take her directly home.

"I'm positive since the coffeehouse stays open all night. I'll call Ian when I get home to let him know it's there."

"Thanks, and thanks for tonight. I had so much fun and the roller-coaster ride was wonderful. I really needed to scream."

He raised a brow as he lowered the volume on the CD player. "You needed to scream?"

A smile touched her lips. "Yes. My stepmother got on my last nerve earlier today and I've been wanting to scream ever since."

Suddenly Wesley's body ached at the thought of another method he could have used to make her scream. He had been too aware of Jasmine tonight. And he was even more aware of her now. Even the sound of her breathing as she sat next to him with her eyes close and her head thrown back, was a total turn-on. His hands tightened on the steering wheel when he remembered how she'd all but jumped into his lap during the ride through the haunted house. She had felt so good in his arms.

"You got a busy day tomorrow?" he asked.

When he came to a traffic light, he watched as she slowly moved her head and opened her eyes to look at him. "I don't have to go into the office but I have a number of personal chores and errands to do. So I'd appreciate it if you let the shadow thing rest for a day."

He chuckled as he moved his gaze back to the road

when the traffic light changed. The thought of not seeing her tomorrow bothered him more than it should have. "I'll think about it. Besides, you'll need me to take you to the coffeehouse tomorrow to get your car."

"No, thanks. I can manage. I'll just ask Ronnie to take me."

His gaze flickered back to her for a quick moment. "Ronnie?"

"Yes, Veronica Strongman, a co-worker and good friend."

Wesley released a deep breath, one he wasn't aware that he'd been holding. At first he had assumed Ronnie was a male and he didn't want to acknowledge the quick stab of jealousy at the thought she was involved with someone. But did she have a man in her life? It was something he'd wondered about since meeting her. Now was as good a time as any to find out.

"What about your boyfriend? Can't he take you to pick it up?"

She chuckled like the question had amused her. "That's not a possibility since I don't have a boyfriend. I don't believe in dating."

She'd said the words with such a firm conviction that Wesley immediately believed her. "Why don't you believe in dating?" he asked more than mildly curious.

"Mainly to keep peace in my family since it seems my stepsisters have a tendency to want anything I have, and they have proven in the past that a boyfriend is no different."

He was glad the car had come to a complete stop

for a train so he could look over at her. "One of your sisters took your boyfriend?"

Even as tired as she was, Jasmine couldn't help but grin at the look of shock on Wesley's face. "Yes, they've done so a couple of times, although now as I look back, they were doing me favors. Especially with one man I had planned to marry by the name of Paul Sanders. But still, it was just the principle of the thing."

Wesley shook his head. Evidently, in addition to there not being any love lost between Jasmine and her stepsisters, there wasn't any loyalty, either. "But why would they do something like that?"

"Because neither of them feel I'm deserving of anything, especially a little love and happiness." She wondered why she was even sharing this information with Wesley. She was obviously more tired than she had thought to be talking so freely about an issue that had caused her such pain two years ago. The only other person who knew about the strained relationship between her stepmother and stepsisters was Ronnie.

"Why didn't you tell your stepmother so she—"

Jasmine cut off his question with outright laughter. "She's the one who orchestrated the entire thing. My fiancé was an attorney and we had set a date to marry. It had really bothered my stepmother from the first that Paul had shown interest in me and not her darling daughters. One day I left to go out of town and she arranged for me to walk in and catch him and Alyssa in a very compromising situation when I returned. I had to applaud my stepmother for her cunning and boo Paul for his weakness. I broke our engagement and walked out the house that day thinking they deserved each other. That's the same day I moved out."

He nodded. "Are Alyssa and Paul still together?"

"No, that happened over two years ago. Alyssa decided that she needed a richer husband than an attorney and has since shifted her sights on greener pastures."

Wesley shook his head, thinking that if he lived to be the ripe old age of one hundred, he still wouldn't be able to figure out the workings of a female mind. Moments later, he pulled into Jasmine's apartment building and brought the car to a stop. "Are you sure you don't need me to take you to get your car tomorrow?"

"Yes, I'm positive," she said, deciding it was best to get out of the car and go inside now that she'd become awake and her awareness of him had doubled. But for some reason, she couldn't move and for an endless moment their gazes met and held.

"Thanks again for tonight. I'll probably sleep like a baby, I'm so exhausted," she said quietly.

He nodded, doubting he would sleep at all no matter how tired he was. "You're welcome, and I had fun, too."

Wesley knew what he wanted to do as he stared at the tumbled mass of braids on her head, the deep darkness of her eyes and the fullness of her lips. This wasn't a dream like he'd had the other night. This was the real thing and they were together, sitting close and their mouths were just inches apart.

Oh, what the hell, he thought as a wave of longing washed over him. He leaned in closer to capture her mouth, knowing he needed to taste her just as much as he needed to breathe.

The moment his mouth connected to hers, a rush of heated desire took over and he slipped his tongue into her mouth as easily as anything he'd ever done. There hadn't been any hesitation; just anticipation for the sweet, sensual taste he'd known awaited him.

Red-hot sensations poured through his bloodstream. He seemed incapable of getting enough of her taste and the little moans emitting from deep in her throat indicated she felt the same way. Her arms reached over and wrapped around his neck, locking his mouth to hers...as if he would go anywhere else. He was right where he wanted to be.

He knew that from this moment on, he would continue to have wonderful dreams about her mouth but never again would he have to wonder about the flavor. It was just as he'd thought, spicy hot with a rich blend of passion and a dose of rapture, of the toe-curling, quick-arousal kind. The interior of the car oozed with sexual chemistry and he was more aware of her than any woman he had ever known. Tonight, right now, control was not an issue—satisfaction was, and feasting on her mouth was giving him satisfaction of the most rewarding kind.

Moments later, when he finally pulled his mouth away, he heard her sigh of disappointment and it matched his groan of frustration. He leaned back against the seat feeling boneless and weak, but two hundred percent gratified. He wondered what were his chances of ever taking her in the back seat of his other cars. Maybe the Mercedes. Just the thought made him aware of just how much he wanted her. He might think differently in the morning after he got his head back on straight, but now, this very minute, he wanted her with a passion that was totally consuming him.

He glanced over at her. She had her eyes closed as she tried to regulate her breathing. He watched as she slowly opened her eyes and looked at him and said. ''That should not have happened, Wesley.''

Somehow he found enough strength to shrug his shoulders. ''But it did.''

She nodded. There was nothing else for her to do but to acknowledge it was true. ''We can't let it happen again.''

He squinted, wondering whom she was trying to convince? Him or her? ''Is that how you feel?'' he asked, wondering if there was a way they could control such a thing from happening again.

She shook her head. ''No, that's not how I feel, since I can't deal with my feelings right now. But that's what I think. We don't like each other. I'm your enemy. I won't stop trying to find out information about Abraham Danforth, if that's what tonight was all about.''

He stared at her. It was probably a good idea if he returned her locket and never saw her again because although she wasn't dealing with her feelings, he was. Emotions he didn't know he had were slamming through him.

''Tonight had nothing to do with Abraham,'' he said, more frustrated with himself than with her. He scowled. Hell, tonight *should* have been about Abraham. Her obsession with finding out information to use against Abraham Danforth was the main reason they had met and why he was shadowing her every day.

"So you won't give up?" he asked, but he already knew what her response would be.

"No."

"Then I'll continue to shadow you, but I will give you a reprieve tomorrow since I have to make a short trip to Brunswick anyway. But tonight was about us, Jasmine and not Abraham. And whether something like that kiss will happen again is up to us."

"We need to keep our relationship on a business level, Wesley. We can't have it both ways."

Without waiting for him to say anything else, Jasmine quickly opened the car door and got out, leaving Wesley sitting in the car thinking of her parting remark.

Five

This shouldn't be happening.

Jasmine decided for the umpteenth time that day when her mind turned once again to Wesley. She had gone to bed last night with him on her mind; she had dreamed about him, and since awakening, her thoughts would drift to him again and again.

She had done most of her errands; had shopped for groceries, paid her bills online, and had checked in with her boss regarding her assignments for the remainder of the week. Still, she had felt the relentless reminders of the evening she and Wesley had shared at the country fair and the kiss they had indulged in when he'd brought her home.

That had been some kiss. It had heated her insides to such a degree that last night, when she had slipped beneath her cool sheets, her body's temperature had warmed the bed linens. And in spite of the little voice inside of her that warned her not to put much stock in the kiss they'd shared, she *was* putting stock into it.

Every time she thought of the way his mouth had expertly taken hers, kissing her in a way she had never been kissed before, she was convinced that for just a little while, Wesley had completely forgotten she was the enemy. For that brief moment she had not been a woman he couldn't trust; a woman he thought was hell-bent on bringing turmoil to the lives of people he considered family.

Even as a nagging voice inside of her reminded her that she and Wesley could not take their relationship any further, she couldn't stop the ripple of pleasure that escalated up her body. For just a little while she wanted to enjoy the memories they'd made last night. She wanted to relive the feel of his hand holding hers as they walked around the fair visiting various booths and the warmth of his breath against her neck when they sat close together in the numerous rides they had tried out.

While they'd watched a performer stick a flaming torch down his throat, Wesley stood so close to her. Jasmine could still smell traces of his aftershave—a masculine and spicy scent he always wore. And last but not least, she could not forget riding the miniature train into the haunted house. Something had grabbed her in the darkness and without thinking, she had practically landed in Wesley's lap. For some reason, she had felt safe being that close to him. The ache that had developed from that encounter was still there, low in her belly.

Jasmine sighed deeply, knowing that she had to be realistic. But she desperately needed a day off from being levelheaded. She wanted to forget that she and Wesley were not supposed to get along. For once she didn't want to be sensible. For just a little while longer she wanted to be a woman who could truly appreciate a fine man.

As she put away the last of her groceries, her sanity finally returned…at least some of it. She still couldn't erase memories of their kiss and the feel of his mouth, hungry, seductive, expertly tasting her and stroking a need deep within in.

Sighing deeply, Jasmine glanced down at her watch. She would be meeting an old high-school friend who was passing through town later that day for dinner. She hoped by the time she returned back home she would have sobered up and erased thoughts of Wesley from her mind completely.

"So what's going on with you, Wes?"

The intensity in Jake Danforth's brown eyes reflected both curiosity and concern. Jake knew him better than anyone and if Jake could detect that something was bothering him then he was really in bad shape.

"Why do you ask?" he responded, leaning back on the sofa and meeting Jake's gaze. He had come straight to Jake's home for dinner after returning from Brunswick. Larissa had taken their son Peter upstairs for his bath and he and Jake were sitting back relaxing after enjoying the delicious meal Larissa had prepared.

"Mainly because you seem preoccupied about something," Jake said. "I talked to Ian today and he mentioned that you whisked Jasmine Carmody away from the coffeehouse before Uncle Abraham arrived."

Wesley nodded. "Yes, and although I'm sure Abraham would have been able to handle an impromptu interview from her, I felt he didn't necessarily need the hassle from a reporter hell-bent on digging into his personal life."

"Well, I'm sure he knew that sort of thing would happen once he decided to run for public office," Jake said, taking a sip of his beer.

Wesley knew that was true but that didn't mean Abraham had to put up with Jasmine's staunch determination to see what dirt she could uncover. Exasperated he checked his watch. It was getting late. He had stayed over at Jake's place longer than he'd planned. A part of him wondered what Jasmine was doing about now. Was she still up or had she gone to bed already? He didn't want to admit it but he had missed shadowing her today and actually looked forward to resuming his routine tomorrow.

"I'm going to call it a night, Jake. Don't forget next week's poker game. Think you can pull yourself away from your family for a few hours?" Wesley asked smiling. Jake had become a regular family man and Wesley could clearly see the love he had for his wife and son.

Jake chuckled. "It will be hard to leave Larissa and Peter, but I'll be there."

On the drive home, Wesley's mind was consumed with thoughts of Jasmine. Something inside of him had stirred last night when she'd shared with him the situation involving her stepmother and stepsisters. He felt fortunate for the close relationship and special bond that he had with Harold, Miranda, Jake and all the other Danforths.

A smile broke onto his features when he thought that no matter what the situation involving Jasmine's family affairs, there was no doubt in his mind that she was handling things the way she saw fit. She was too much of a headstrong female not to.

He remembered how she had met his gaze head-on, her eyes had filled with all-fire anger, when he had announced that he would become her shadow. He had known then that if pushed hard enough she would come out scratching, and that she would be a worthy opponent, both in and out of the bedroom. A part of him was dying to see how he could unleash that fiery side of her in bed.

He sighed, wondering if Jasmine had cast some sort of spell on him. When it came to her, he was definitely not in full control of his senses. There was something about her that seemed to ignite his blood. Spending time with her last night at the country fair hadn't helped matters.

Wearing a pullover blouse and skirt, her clothing had definitely complemented her long, lithe, delectable curves and a few times he had wondered if he would be able to survive her proximity. Once or twice he had noticed her watching him and had wondered what she'd been thinking.

Even now he could picture her home, curled up in bed wearing something outrageously sexy, something that aroused him just thinking about it.

Wesley cursed beneath his breath when he was suddenly consumed with the need to talk to Jasmine, to hear her voice. He heaved a rough sigh when he picked up his cell phone and punched in the phone number he'd already memorized. Convincing himself that he was only checking up on her to make sure she had stuck to her plans to take care of personal errands and not stick her nose anywhere it didn't belong, he listened as her phone rang.

He felt his body tense when she didn't answer. He was about to end the call when he heard her pick up the phone.

"Hello?" Her voice sounded out of breath.

Wesley felt his body relax. "Where were you?" he asked, too harshly even for his own ears.

"And what's it to you?" she answered smartly.

Wesley smiled. It seemed that she hadn't lost that sweet-tempered, mild-mannered disposition of hers. "I was just checking to make sure you got through today without getting into trouble."

He heard her unladylike snort. "If you mean did I do any checking into Abraham Danforth then the answer is no. But you may as well know that I plan to pay him a visit first thing tomorrow. There's a rumor floating around that someone tried to sabotage his computer, which I'm sure you already know about.''

Wesley frowned, wondering where she had heard that from and not liking the fact that she was close to the truth. But there was no way he would let her know that. ''Abraham's computer merely picked up some sort of virus. That can happen to any computer. Besides, that was weeks ago. I would think that was old news.''

''Yes, but it has come up again that someone has it in for him and I want to know who.'' Jasmine decided not to tell Wesley about the phone call she had received from her boss, Manny, indicating someone had called the newspaper with a tip that stated the truth about Abraham Danforth's true character would be revealed soon. Of course Manny wanted them to be the one to do the headline story, no matter what it was.

''Back off, Jasmine.''

She heard the anger in Wesley's voice and decided to ignore it. ''I'm just doing the job that I'm getting paid to do, Wesley. Now if you don't mind, I'd like to end this conversation since my floor is getting wet.''

''Why?'' he asked flustered, angered.

Jasmine raised a brow. ''Why what?''

''Why is your floor getting wet?''

Jasmine tossed her braids back, away from her face. ''Because at the time you called, I was in the shower. Thinking this was a very important phone call, I rushed out without grabbing a towel.''

Something deep within Wesley stirred to life. The mere thought of Jasmine standing in the middle of the floor without a stitch of clothing covering her body made him feel heated, hot, aroused. He reached up to loosen his tie and shifted his position in the car.

A part of him wondered if she enjoyed rattling his senses, stirring up his emotions and kicking his hormones into overdrive. He knew that to deal with Jasmine Carmody he would have to keep a tight rein on his mental faculties and remain detached, no matter how hard it would be.

"Then I guess I'd better let you go."

"I'd appreciate it." Then without waiting for him to say goodbye, she ended the call.

The following day Wesley stood a few feet away watching Jasmine. One minute, he had been thinking he had gotten his head back on straight regarding her, then the next he was more confused than ever. This was one of those times.

Jasmine was standing on the steps of the courthouse interviewing the man who had just announced he was throwing his hat into the ring in the mayoral race. A small crowd had gathered and she was one of several reporters present. He was so focused on her he only half heard the questions she was asking.

Instead, he was too busy scanning her features. They were serious, intent and beautiful enough to take your breath away. He wondered if she was aware of just how sexy she looked dressed in a beige silk blouse and a chocolate brown straight skirt that stopped above her knees.

It dawned on him that the interview session was

over when the crowd began dispersing. She turned, met his gaze and froze. He watched her brown eyes grow wary, aggravated, agitated.

It seemed they were back to square one.

But maybe not. There had been a kiss; a kiss he couldn't forget and he doubted that she could, either. Knowing she had intended to interview Abraham this morning, he was about to save her the trouble from driving across town to Crofthaven by letting her know that Abraham had left town that morning on a business trip, but decided not to. Chances are she would not have believed him anyway.

He watched as she slowly made her way down the courthouse steps and decided to meet her halfway. When they met, coming face-to-face, he placed his hands in his pockets to keep from reaching out and touching her, or pulling her into his arms and kissing her again. "Jasmine," he acknowledged.

"Wesley," she acknowledged back. "Don't you ever get tired of following me around?"

Wesley heard the irritation in her voice. "I gave you a break yesterday."

"No thanks for small favors. Don't you think we should handle this another way? I feel like I'm being spied on."

He smiled at that. "Now you know how Abraham must feel at times."

She narrowed her gaze at him. "He's running for public office, I'm not."

"That's a good enough reason for your unfair treatment of him? I don't see you snooping around his opponent, John Van Gelder.''

Jasmine made a low sound of frustration before saying. ''I'm not being unfair to Abraham Danforth. I'm assigned to cover him, not Van Gelder.''

Wesley crossed his arms over his chest. ''An assignment that was very unlucky for the Danforth family.''

She sighed. ''I regret they feel that way. Now if you'll excuse me, I need to make it to my next interview.''

When she walked off, Wesley couldn't help noticing how nicely her skirt stretched across her backside, a very delectable-looking backside. And he couldn't stop himself from thinking about how the sexy curve of that backside would feel against him.

When he had gotten home last night, images of her naked, standing in the middle of the bedroom while talking to him on the phone had taken over his mind. Trying to get some work done had been out of the question and he'd ended up taking his own shower and going to bed.

But he hadn't been able to sleep. All he could do was think about her. Instead of locking horns with her, he wanted them to lock bodies. He'd tossed and turned in bed all night. Who would have thought that one kiss would have driven him to such a state? One kiss and he was dying for another one. The thought of never kissing her again was tying his stomach into knots.

He sighed deeply. Although the sun was out, the air

was sharp and chill, unusual for a Savannah day in April. But then he needed the sharp chill to ward off the heat in his body. It was a heat he could not get rid of thanks to Jasmine.

Jasmine snapped her cell phone closed and placed it back in her purse. She had finished her last interview for the day and was headed home. She had awakened that morning with high hopes of interviewing Abraham Danforth but he had left town unexpectedly on a business trip. The reporter in her wondered what had been so urgent about the trip to Atlanta and why he'd gone instead of his son Ian, who was now in charge of the business.

She was about to exit off the interstate but a quick glance in her rearview mirror showed Wesley's car was following in the lane behind her.

She sighed in frustration. The man was getting on her last nerve. She glanced at her watch. It was still early and if Wesley was determined to shadow her every activity then she wouldn't make things easy on him. Actually, she hoped to make things nearly impossible. She hadn't finished doing all her errands yesterday and decided now was a good time to complete that task and hoped that Wesley was up for it. She glanced back in the rearview mirror and smiled. First she would stop by the dry cleaners, then the car wash, and from there she would go to the butcher and the florist to pick out a plant to sit on her desk.

If the man had nothing better to do with his time than follow her around, that was his business.

What in the hell was the woman up to? Wesley wondered a short while later as he continued to follow her. She had told him she would be taking care of most of her errands yesterday, but so far she had made five stops at various places, parking her car, going into stores and either coming out with nothing or little at all. He released a frustrated sigh but was determined to stay on her tail.

He heard his stomach growl, reminding him it was past dinnertime yet here he was, sitting in the parking lot of Wal-Mart waiting for Jasmine to come out. Moments later, she walked out carrying a small bag. But the bag wasn't what caught his attention. Once again his gaze was drawn to her skirt and how it stretched against her bottom, and the way her hips swiveled when she walked. Damn. Sexual frustration was taking a toll on him and there was no excuse for it when all he had to do was to pick up his phone and call any number of women who'd be glad to relieve him. But he wasn't interested in any other woman other than the one crossing the parking lot at that very moment.

He closed his eyes and tried to remember that the woman was Jasmine Carmody. Jasmine the piranha of a reporter. Jasmine who was determined to dig up dirt on those he cared about. But then he also was reminded that she was Jasmine, the woman he had kissed senseless a couple of nights ago.

When he opened his eyes she had gotten into her car and was driving off. He hoped she was heading home but when she turned her vehicle in the opposite direction of her home, he knew that was not the case. *Didn't she plan on going home at some point today?*

Forty minutes later and she was finally headed toward home. It had taken Wesley a few hours to figure out just what Jasmine had been doing and the game she'd been playing with him.

He frowned. If she thought the joke was on him she had another thought coming. If nothing else, he had shown her that he intended to stick to her like glue. Eventually, she would realize that he was not someone she could toy with.

An hour later, Wesley opened the door to his home at the same time his answering machine clicked on. ''Wes, this is Kim. Give me a call when you get in. Zack and I want to invite you over for dinner tomorrow night.''

Wes smiled when he heard Kim's voice. He was glad Abraham's daughter, Kim, had found Zack, a man to give her the love and happiness she deserved.

He would call her back and confirm dinner after his shower—a shower he needed to calm his overheated body. At this point whether he was hot from anger or sexual frustration he wasn't sure. All he knew at the moment was that one part of him wanted to put his hands around Jasmine's neck while another part of him wanted to put his hands on other parts of her.

A few minutes later he was stepping inside the shower stall and under the spray of cold water in an effort to quell the sexual tension and anger that had overtaken him most of the evening. Since getting home, nothing he'd done had helped him to relax.

The Silhouette Reader Service™ — Here's how it works:

Accepting your 2 free books and gift places you under no obligation to buy anything. You may keep the books and gift and return the shipping statement marked "cancel." If you do not cancel, about a month later we'll send you 6 additional books and bill you just $3.57 each in the U.S., or $4.24 each in Canada, plus 25¢ shipping & handling per book and applicable taxes if any.* That's the complete price and — compared to cover prices of $4.25 each in the U.S. and $4.99 each in Canada — it's quite a bargain! You may cancel at any time, but if you choose to continue, every month we'll send you 6 more books, which you may either purchase at the discount price or return to us and cancel your subscription.

*Terms and prices subject to change without notice. Sales tax applicable in N.Y. Canadian residents will be charged applicable provincial taxes and GST.

PLAY Lucky 7

and get 2 FREE BOOKS and a FREE GIFT

DETACH AND MAIL CARD TODAY!

Scratch off the gold area with a coin. Then check below to see the gifts you get!

NO COST! NO OBLIGATION TO BUY! NO PURCHASE NECESSARY!

YES! I have scratched off the gold area. Please send me the **2 FREE BOOKS AND GIFT** for which I qualify. I understand I am under no obligation to purchase any books as explained on the back of this card.

326 SDL DZ4W   225 SDL DZ5D

FIRST NAME	LAST NAME

ADDRESS

APT.#	CITY

STATE/PROV.   ZIP/POSTAL CODE   (S-D-04/04)

7 7 7	Worth **2 FREE BOOKS** plus a **FREE GIFT!**
🍒🍒🍒	Worth **2 FREE BOOKS!**
♣♣♣	Worth **1 FREE BOOK!**
🔔🔔🍒	Try Again!

Warning bells went off in his head. No woman had ever affected him this way and he didn't like it worth a damn. By the time he had finished his shower and dried off, he decided he would spend a quiet evening at home reading. He was determined not to indulge in foolish fantasies like he'd done the night before.

Drawing in a calming breath he walked downstairs. He'd eaten dinner, but there was another hunger deep within him. He needed to get a firm grip or he was going to be in serious trouble.

He was about to walk outside on the terrace when he heard the doorbell. Remembering he had left his security gate unlocked, he figured his visitor was probably Jake. He made his way to the door and opened it to find Abraham Danforth standing there instead.

"Abraham, come in," Wesley greeted, smiling. He'd always had deep respect and admiration for Abraham Danforth and knew that his political aspirations were genuine and sincere.

Wesley knew that Abraham truly loved his children, but he also acknowledged that following the death of Abraham's wife in an automobile accident, the young widower had felt unable to give them the care they needed. Ian had told him that Abraham had sent them all off to boarding schools. He knew that Ian still held a lot of resentment regarding his childhood years of having to spend much of his youth trying to impress his father and feeling that he had failed to do so.

"Hi, Wes, I hope I'm not catching you at a bad time."

"No, not at all," Wesley said. From the first time

he had met Abraham, he'd always seen the same depth of kindness and caring in Abraham's blue eyes that was always there in his brother Harold's. "Can I get you anything to drink?" he asked.

Abraham shook his head. "No, I'm fine. I got a message that you wanted to see me. I just got back from a short trip to Atlanta."

Wesley nodded. "I was wondering if you've received any more threatening e-mails?"

A few months ago, three separate e-mails had been sent to Abraham through his computer. Each had contained a cryptic message and had been signed "Lady Savannah."

The first e-mail had read, "I've been watching you." The second, "I'm still watching you." The last e-mail that had read, "Expect the unexpected. This isn't over," and had contained a virus that had wiped out Abraham's entire computer system. Because of the signature, everyone was assuming the person who had sent the e-mails was a woman and was wondering why she was targeting Abraham. The only people who knew about the e-mails were members of the Danforth family and they intended to keep it that way. The last thing they wanted was for the information to get leaked to the media. He could just imagine what Jasmine would do with information like that at her disposal. Abraham had hired a security specialist to secretly work on the case by the name of Michael Whittaker.

Abraham shook his head. "No, not since the last

one that crashed my computer. I'm glad you were able to repair it for me.''

"I was glad to do it," Wesley stated, leaning against his closed door.

The older man studied Wesley for a few moments then asked, ''Is that all you had to talk to me about, Wes? For some reason I think there's more.''

Wesley smiled. Just like Harold, Abraham could read him like a book at times. "Yes, there is something else. A woman by the name of Jasmine Carmody. I'm sure you probably know her by now.''

Abraham chuckled as he nodded. "Ah, yes, Ms. Carmody. She is a very dedicated reporter who can be relentless in her interviews. Although I have to admit she gets rather intense at times, I know she is merely doing her job.''

Wesley knew Abraham had stated things as diplomatically as he could. "She mentioned to me today that she heard your computer had gotten sabotaged and wanted to question you about it. I just thought I'd let you know. I also wanted you to know that she was rummaging through my garbage last week looking for anything that I may have tossed out after repairing your computer. Since I see she's intent on getting into trouble, I've decided to keep a close eye on her.''

Abraham shrugged. "Although I'm as anxious as everyone else to know how Martha died, I have nothing to hide, Wes, so she can do all the digging that she wants.'' The older man then studied Wesley intently. "But I am concerned about you.''

Wesley raised a brow. "Me? Why?''

Abraham studied Wesley for a few moments before speaking. "Because I know how you feel about female reporters and I don't want you to think every one of them is like that young woman you dated in college. I know what a difficult time that was for you. It's not always easy when a person's trust has been betrayed." He was quiet a moment and then added, "I often worry about you and Ian. The two of you have been hurt by women, and I don't want the two of you to let it ever stop you from experiencing true love and happiness."

An hour after Abraham left, Wesley was still thinking about the older man's words. He couldn't speak for Ian, but as far as he was concerned, there was no such thing as true love and happiness when it came to a woman.

There wasn't any woman that he wanted to share his life with and he intended to keep it that way.

Six

Jasmine stared at her car not believing what she saw. Of all things, she had a flat tire. She tried to remember what she had learned in that auto mechanics class she and Ronnie had taken a few years ago, and couldn't recall much of anything. And when she tried using her mobile phone to call for road service, she had discovered her phone battery was low and she couldn't make the call.

She had just come from a press conference at Crofthaven. The coroner's report had ruled that Martha Jones, whose body had been identified in the attic last week, had died of a heart attack. It seemed that Martha had had a congenital heart condition and had run away from home several times in the past. From what the authorities had been able to piece together, after a heated argument with her overly protective mother, at the age of sixteen Martha had gone to the attic to hide out when she'd suffered a fatal heart attack. Since that part of the house was never used, Martha's body had gone undiscovered for three years.

Jasmine sighed and glanced around. There weren't too many cars traveling by and those who'd passed hadn't slowed down to offer help. Thinking she would save time getting home, she had decided to use the two-lane stretch of road instead of the interstate to avoid rush-hour traffic. Now she didn't like the thought of being stranded.

Maybe if she took a look at the tools she had in the trunk, she might recall how to change a tire. She went to the back of her car and began pulling out her jack and spare tire.

When she heard the sound of a vehicle pulling up, she nervously glanced over her shoulder. She was alone on a practically deserted stretch of highway. Releasing the jack from her hand she gripped her key chain that also held her pepper spray.

Ready to take aim if she had to, she turned quickly and exhaled a deep sigh of relief when she saw it was Wesley. She didn't think she could be happier to see him.

"Need help?"

She shook her head. "Yes, please. I've got a flat tire. Do you know how to change one?"

He grinned. "Of course. If you need transportation for another interview, you can take my car and I'll take care of things here and bring your car to you later."

She glanced at his elegant silver-gray Mercedes and

thought his offer was more than generous. "No, I'm all through for today and was on my way home. I tried calling road service but my cell-phone battery is low."

"No problem. I'll take over from here. If you'd like, you can go sit in my car and turn on the air conditioner. It's getting pretty hot out here." He couldn't help noticing how her blouse had become damp and was beginning to stick to her perfectly shaped breasts. Today she was wearing a pair of slacks so he couldn't see the gorgeous legs he'd thought about so often.

"No, I'm fine. Besides, I need to watch what you're doing so I can learn what to do the next time."

He met her gaze as he moved toward her trunk. "I hope there's not a next time." He meant it. He didn't like the idea of her being stranded on an isolated stretch of road with a flat tire. He would have come by sooner had he not been talking with Harold and Miranda Danforth.

He'd considered them his unofficial adoptive parents for the past fourteen years. Miranda had been scolding him about looking too thin and not eating enough. He had decided to use the two-lane highway instead of the interstate due to rush-hour traffic and was glad that he had. He didn't want to think how long Jasmine might have been stranded had he not come by.

"I hope there's not a next time, too, but I still want to watch," she said moving out of his way when he pulled out the jack and spare tire.

A few moments later she regretted watching Wesley. She barely paid any attention to what he was doing. He had removed his jacket and rolled up his shirtsleeves. She couldn't help noticing his powerful arms and broad shoulders and the way his slacks stretched tight across his muscular thighs as he removed the flat tire.

Less than fifteen minutes later, he was done. "That about does it, but you should get this tire fixed sometime tomorrow."

"I will and thanks for your help. What do I owe you?"

"Nothing," he said, placing the flat tire in her trunk. "Just make sure you get this repaired tomorrow."

Jasmine nodded, then remembered she'd been planning to cook spaghetti for dinner. Wesley was used to eating the microwave kind and she wondered if he would appreciate eating the real thing for once. She made a quick decision to find out.

"I'm cooking spaghetti tonight. I know how much you like it and wondered if you'd like to join me?"

"For dinner?" he asked, raising a brow as he closed down the trunk.

"Yes, for dinner. Nothing fancy, just spaghetti and a salad."

Wesley paused. He could think of no reason why he shouldn't join her for dinner other than the one nagging him. He didn't want spaghetti and a salad—he wanted her.

"Yes, I'd like to join you for dinner. Thanks for the invitation."

"Thanks for your help just now. Do you want to follow me home?"

He glanced down at himself. He looked rumpled

and felt sweaty. "I'd like to go home, shower and change first."

"All right and I'll go on home and start dinner." A smile spread across her lips before she opened her car door.

"I'll follow you."

She lifted a brow. "Why? You fixed my tire."

"Yes, but I still want to make sure you get home safely. On rare occasions, spares have been known to go flat, too."

She nodded. "Should I expect you at my place in an hour or so?"

The smile she gave him had hit him right in the groin. "Yes, that would be the right time."

He began walking back to his car as she started the engine to her vehicle thinking that that shower he intended to take needed to be a cold one.

Wesley smelled the delicious aroma of spaghetti sauce the moment he walked into Jasmine's home.

"I hope you're hungry since I made a huge pot," Jasmine said, closing the door behind him.

She tried to ignore how good he looked in a pair of jeans and a pullover shirt. She recalled the first time she had seen him in jeans—that night he had appeared out of the darkness while she'd been going through his trash. And then, like now, she thought he looked utterly sexy.

"I've never known spaghetti to go to waste while I'm around," Wesley said in an amused voice, breaking into her thoughts.

Jasmine couldn't help but smile. "Good. You can

come straight to the kitchen where I have everything set up. I thought it would be nice to sit on my screened-in patio. Although I don't have a view of the Savannah River like you do, I have a view of a lake that I think is rather nice.''

''I'm sure it is.'' His smile widened when he walked into her kitchen. It was almost as large as his but definitely better equipped. He liked the way she had things set up, including the way several pots hung from a pot rack.

''You can wash your hands in that bathroom across the hall while I get things ready on the patio.''

The cold shower hadn't done him any good, Wesley thought as he went into the bathroom to wash his hands. He couldn't get over how good she looked in a pair of shorts and a tank top. Like him, she had decided to dress comfortably for dinner. And yet the casual outfit still managed to turn him on.

When he returned to the kitchen she was loading everything on a serving tray. ''There's a wine rack around the corner in the area that separates the kitchen from the dining area. How about selecting us a bottle?''

''Do you have a preference?'' he asked.

''No, whatever you'd like.''

He decided to select a red wine—one he knew was delicious with pasta. When he joined her on the patio, she had set the table and the spaghetti was served in a beautiful ceramic pasta platter. He smiled when he saw she had also baked a batch of garlic bread and he had a feeling it would taste as good as it looked.

"Everything is ready, so sit down and help your-self."

He did, however, he waited for her to serve herself and say grace before digging in. "Umm…this is de-licious," he said moments later after taking his first forkful."

"Thanks."

"Who taught you how to cook?"

"My aunt. I went to live with her for a while after my mom died. She loved to cook and together we would try out a lot of dishes."

"How long did you live with her?"

"Less than six months. My father loved my mother very much and he took her death extremely hard. He needed to go through that period of mourning alone. I think the only reason he remarried was because he thought he was doing me a favor."

Although she didn't say anything else, Wesley knew from what Jasmine had shared with him the other night that her father had unknowingly done her a disservice instead of a favor. It didn't take much for him to gather that the woman her father had married was the stepmother from hell.

"Is your aunt still living?"

Jasmine shook her head. "No, she died five years ago."

The sadness in her voice touched him. "Other than your father, do you have any other family?"

"No, he was an only child and my mother had that one sister who never had any children of her own," she said thinking of her aunt Rena.

Wesley said nothing for a moment, and then said. "Your mother was a very beautiful woman."

She met his gaze, surprised. "How do you know?"

"The locket."

She didn't say anything for a long moment as she looked into his hazel eyes. She had almost forgotten about the locket and that he still had it. "Yes, she was beautiful."

"You favor her."

Jasmine's breath caught as their gazes held. For a moment she wasn't sure how to respond. His compliment had caught her off guard.

"Thank you," she finally said softly.

Wesley and Jasmine enjoyed the rest of their meal while discussing various topics, steering clear of Abraham Danforth and the press conference he'd held earlier that day. However, they did talk about the rumor that had been going around for years that Crofthaven was haunted.

Wesley smiled as he finished off the last of his spaghetti. "I've spent a number of nights at Crofthaven and have never seen this ghost people claim is there. However, Reid and Jake swear it exists."

Jasmine lifted a brow. "Reid? That's Abraham's second oldest son, right? The one who's getting married in a few months."

"Yes. Reid and Tina Morgan are getting married and everyone is excited about it." He took a sip of his wine before continuing. "Dinner was wonderful and I appreciate the invitation."

"I'm glad you could join me. And I really appreciate your help in changing that tire. I'm glad you came along when you did. I was beginning to get a little nervous on that road alone.'' She then took a glance at the darkening sky. ''I think we might get a thunderstorm tonight.''

Wesley stood. ''Then I'd better help you with dishes so I can be on my way.''

''You don't have to help with dishes, Wesley.''

He chuckled. ''Hey, no arguing. It's the least I can do after enjoying such a delicious meal.''

Jasmine laughed. ''Okay, if you insist, but remember I told you that I could do them by myself.''

''I'll remember but I think four hands will be better than two.''

She washed and he dried while he told her about his Internet sales company and how it got started. He had capitalized on the contacts he had made in college, and she could tell the Danforths had been supportive. This explained his fierce loyalty to the Danforths and why he considered them as his family. In a way she understood because she was fiercely loyal to her father, as well.

''Well, that about does it with the dishes,'' she said, putting the last one away. ''If you'd like, I can prepare you a bowl of spaghetti to take with you since I have so much left.''

''Are you sure?''

She smiled. ''Yes, I'm positive. It won't take but a second.''

He leaned back against the counter as he watched her spoon a hefty portion of spaghetti into a large bowl and then wrapped it with clear cling wrap. She also wrapped up a few pieces of garlic bread. After bagging up both, she placed the bag in the middle of the table. It was then that they heard the raindrops beginning to fall and a quick glance out the window indicated the clouds had been much closer than they'd thought. The rain was already coming down fast and furious.

"Maybe you should wait until the rain stops," she said. She walked over to the window and looked out. "It's a mess out there."

"Then if you don't mind, I'll just wait a while."

She turned around and met his gaze. "I don't mind," she said quietly. She shivered slightly either from the chill that had entered the room or from the way Wesley was looking at her.

He saw her tremble and crossed the room. "You're shivering. Are you cold?"

"A little."

He reached out and pulled her into his arms, wrapping her in those big powerful arms she had admired earlier when he'd been changing her tire. "This feel better?" he asked. The question had been whispered close to her ear and sent more shivers through her body. Shivers that he felt.

"You're still shivering," he said softly. "Maybe I should light your fireplace to warm you up some."

When he released her, Jasmine looked into his hazel eyes, tempted to tell him that her shivers had nothing to do with the temperature in the room and had everything to do with him.

A fierce storm may have been raging outside but here, inside her kitchen, deep within her body, another storm was raging. This one was just as turbulent as the one outdoors. And it wasn't helping matters that he was looking at her like she was something he wanted to eat.

"Lighting the fireplace isn't necessary," she said softly, barely able to get the words out.

"Would you rather we sit in your living room on the sofa?" he asked, not taking his eyes from her as his fingertips grazed the smoothness of her arm.

His touch was sending sensations escalating through her entire body and the only thing she could do was nod. Wesley removed his arm from around her shoulders and extended his hand to her. She took it and they walked through the kitchen to the living room. He sat down on the sofa then pulled her down into his lap.

She gasped in surprise and felt the heat of his gaze when she looked at him.

"Relax and let me warm you," he said softly, snuggling her closer into his arms. She felt the moistness of his breath against her forehead.

She sighed, deciding to give in and let him hold her while the rain beat down on the roof. Nothing was said between them as they sat listening to the sound of the thunderstorm and watching the occasional flash of lightning. Jasmine had never been afraid of storms, but for some reason, she appreciated the fact she was not alone—more so that Wesley was the one with her, holding her tight in his arms as if there was no other place he'd rather be.

The room was quiet, except for the sound of the storm and their even breathing. Then she suddenly noticed Wesley's breathing wasn't even anymore. It was beginning to come out choppy and rough. She noted the change the exact moment she felt the hard bulge in his pants press against her bottom.

A warm sensation slithered slowly up her spine and she shifted in his arms, lifted her face from his chest and looked at him. Their gazes locked, and slowly, lifting her mouth to his seemed the most natural thing to do.

He met her halfway, capturing her mouth, stealing whatever breath she had and kissing her as deeply as anyone could be kissed. His tongue probed, coaxed, and delivered a sudden throbbing between her thighs.

The kiss claimed everything within her—every thought, every sigh and every moan. Then it created greed, a need and a hunger for something she'd never had but desperately wanted. His tongue was hot, seductive, rapacious, pleasuring her senseless, growling with an urgency that could not be contained.

"I love the way you taste," Wesley murmured, breaking the kiss long enough to lick her jaw, throat and lips. "I haven't forgotten it since that night."

She hadn't forgotten his taste, either, she wanted to say but couldn't find her voice. Her pulse increased when he gently bit the flesh near her shoulder, softly branding her. He slipped his hand under her top to caress her breasts through the thin material of her bra and she let out a deep moan. She had never experienced anything like this. She inhaled deeply when he lifted her top and unsnapped the front closure of her bra, baring her breasts to his gaze.

"You're beautiful." The words poured from deep within Wesley's throat as he looked at her breasts, driven with a need to taste her all over. Her breasts were firm, high and the nipples were dark, inviting, enticing and he bent his head to taste her.

His tongue teased her for endless moments. Then he moved on to the other nipple, delivering the same wonderful torment. Jasmine clutched the back of his head to hold his mouth to her breasts.

Wesley's body responded to her like a schoolboy's. She stirred feelings within him that he'd never felt before. Suddenly, kissing her and tasting her breasts weren't enough. He wanted it all. He was consumed with a hot hunger that was burning deep within him and he needed only what she could give. He lifted his head and met her gaze, focusing sharply on her, needing to see her expression, her reaction to his next words.

"I want to make love to you."

Jasmine returned his gaze and he didn't move. He barely breathed as he waited for her response. He could tell she was thinking, accepting the fact that making love to him would change everything between them. The question of the hour was, was she ready for that? Was he?

He had to make her understand and he reached out and touched his fingertips to her lips. "I don't have all the answers, Jasmine. I don't want to consider the 'what-ifs.' All I know is that now, this very moment, I need and want you in a way I've never needed or wanted a woman before," he whispered huskily.

"I want to go inside you so deep so that I'll know the heat of you and all your glorious warmth. I want to give us pleasure and fulfill our every desire. Will you let me?"

Blood rushed through Jasmine's veins and she wanted Wesley to claim her in a way no man ever had. She didn't want to think of the questions left unanswered or the 'what-ifs,' either. What she wanted was this night, this time with him. Tomorrow she would deal with the rest.

She wanted to concentrate on the man who held her in his arms; the man who was making her grateful that she was a woman.

And she gave him the only response she could. "I want you to make love to me, too, Wesley," she whispered.

A slow smile touched his lips and she felt her stomach clench with a need that almost made it impossible for her to breathe. Cradling her body into the warmth of his arms, he eased to his feet. Her arms looped around his neck, she lowered his mouth down to hers, needing to taste him again; the feelings he evoked within her were overpowering.

He parted her lips and took control of the kiss urgently as he clung to the last bit of his sanity. He slowly lifted his head to ask, "Where's the bedroom?"

She could barely get the words out to answer. "Ahead on your right."

With long strides, Wesley didn't waste any time making it to her bedroom. He glanced around, quickly admiring the décor before placing her in the middle of the huge, white oak sleigh bed. Jasmine lay against the pillow and watched him. He wanted her so much that he could barely think straight. He felt all his self-control dissolving and he couldn't do a damn thing about it.

He sank down on the bed before her and began removing her clothes. After removing the sandals from her feet, he caressed the smooth silkiness of her legs. Moments later he removed her top and bra and when she lifted her hips, he slipped his hands beneath them to pull down her shorts, leaving her clothed in a pair of black lace panties.

He slipped his fingers beneath the waistband of her panties and slowly eased them down her body. He leaned back on his haunches thinking she was the most beautiful woman he had ever seen. Everything about her took his breath away.

Her eyes were on him as he stood and began removing his clothes—which turned him on even more. Although she didn't utter a single word, the look in her eyes urged him to hurry. That same heat and excitement surging through her also slammed into him but he wanted to take things slow and savor every sensuous minute.

Moments later he stood before her gloriously naked, his rich chestnut-colored body was totally male, utterly impressive and fully aroused.

He joined her on the bed and kissed her deeply, mating his tongue with hers the same way he intended for their bodies to mate. He felt his blood pound through his veins as she kissed him back, and her body trembled with the force of her emotions.

His fingers slipped between her legs and felt her heat, her moist desire. He began stroking her as he watched her pupils darken with need.

He needed to know her taste.

In one smooth move, he lowered his head and pulled her against his mouth as his hungry tongue went straight for her center. She jerked at the intimate contact and her fingers clutched the bedspread and lifted her hips for greater connection.

Jasmine thought she was going to lose her mind. Nothing should bring a person such astounding pleasure, such mind-curling enjoyment, she thought incoherently. She moaned deep within her throat as she moved her hips frantically, urgently against his mouth while her fingernails dug deep into his shoulders.

Then suddenly, the tension shattered within her and she cried out, arching her body closer to him, letting herself go and coming apart. She screamed out his name as he tongue-stroked her to sweet oblivion.

Jasmine heard the sound of foil tearing as she fought for breath. Then Wesley moved over her and she felt the heat of him sink slowly into her. She watched as his forehead creased when he encountered resistance. His head dropped back as he breathed deeply and tried to push forward.

Her fingernails dug into his shoulders at the pain and when he lowered his head and met her gaze, she knew that he knew. The look on his face told it all. Their gazes locked for what seemed like an eternity. She felt his hesitation, sensed his resistance and was aware of his inner struggle. She had to let him know that no matter what, she wanted this. She needed this.

Reaching up she wiped the sweat from his forehead and leaned up slightly to claim his mouth and kissed him.

Her tongue mated with his, restoring his passion and shattering his willpower. She felt his muscles tighten, his body flex. When he pushed harder, breaking through, she cried out and he absorbed her cry with his breath.

A moment later her pain subsided and she began returning his kiss. He slowly began moving inside of her and she felt it all the way to her bones. He ignited her pleasure with every smooth stroke. Heat raced to every part of her body and she surrendered to what her body—and his—demanded. And when he increased the tempo, advanced their rhythm to another beat, she tightened her feminine muscles around him, savoring the pleasure.

Her eyes burned with desire when he released her mouth and gazed down at her. "Now, Wesley!"

Her words urged him forward and he thrust into her one last time as their world exploded and pleasure consumed their minds and their bodies. His cry of satisfaction mingled with hers and his body continued to shiver long after the climax had passed.

For several long moments, Wesley held her in his arms. She had drifted off to sleep and he was enjoying just watching her. The only sign that she was still alive was her breathing. At rest, Jasmine looked younger. She was beautiful, special and...*his.*

And she had been a virgin.

He had never made love to a virgin before. When he had realized she was innocent he had tried to withdraw from such unfamiliar territory, uncharted waters. Any thought of turning back deserted him when he'd felt her inner muscles contract around him, claiming him, and he had given her what she wanted. What he wanted. He hadn't believed he could find such pleasure in any woman's arms. No woman had ever given him such a beautiful and special gift. Wesley felt a degree of possessiveness that he'd never felt before.

He swallowed hard when he thought of Caroline. His heart had been broken once and he didn't intend for it to get broken again. But a part of him had to finally admit there was something about Jasmine that was totally different from Caroline Perry.

He had felt it that night they'd gone to the country fair, as well as the few times he'd watched her doing interviews. Getting a big story was her obsession but not her passion. He had reached that conclusion after reading the article she had written about that teacher who'd returned from Iraq. The story had been well written and uplifting. It had generated warmth and human interest.

Yet there was something driving her to go after the kind of stories that were laced with controversy and scandal, stories that could cripple a person's reputation for life.

And as he gathered her closer, he was determined to find out what was driving Jasmine Carmody.

There was a man in her bed.

Jasmine slowly opened her eyes to find her body entwined with Wesley's. Then she remembered the flat tire. Dinner. The thunderstorm. Their lovemaking. She glanced at the clock on the nightstand next to her bed. It was almost one in the morning.

A surge of sensations suddenly swept through her,

filling her with honeyed warmth. When she thought of all the intimacies she and Wesley had shared, she should have felt downright scandalous, but it was very difficult to feel that way when her entire body already wanted more.

She remembered how her body had strained yet adjusted to Wesley. He'd held her hips in place while stroking her relentlessly, penetrating deeper, longer and harder when her inner muscles had relaxed, until he'd been embedded fully within her.

Like he was now.

Heat traveled up her body when she realized he was once again sheathed inside of her, their bodies intimately connected. She moaned deep in her throat and when she felt him getting harder. She met his gaze the moment his eyes opened.

He didn't say anything. Neither did she. They just continued to look at each other as he filled her body with what she needed and wanted.

"It's too soon," he broke the silence and whispered. "We need to—"

He never finished what he was about to say when she thrust her hips against him, wrapped her legs around him, locking their bodies together. "We need to do this again," she said flatly. She wanted him again—now. She clutched his shoulders and her hips began moving in a slow, soul-stirring rhythm that was meant to seduce.

He crushed his mouth to hers, kissing her in a way that made her toes curl and her womanly core melt. When he began moving his body, she forgot all about her body's soreness and concentrated on the frantic pace of their lovemaking as he rocked her with immense pleasure.

Her fingernails sank deeper into his shoulders and she pulled her mouth from his. "Please don't stop," she whispered through a hissed breath, thinking she was about to die. If she was going to take her last breath she couldn't imagine going out any other way.

"I won't," he whispered back, increasing the pace, his body responding to her request. He had wanted to give her tenderness but she had wanted fire. He intended to send her up in smoke. He knew and accepted that he was doing more than making love to her. He was claiming her as his. He didn't want to think about the implications of that.

Now was not the time. This was not the place.

Wesley reached down and filled his hands with her breasts, wanting to be connected to her in every way. He again increased the pace, the tempo wild, furious, unrestrained. And when she cried out his name before the explosion ripped through him, he gripped her hips and went deeper as her quivering muscles pulled at him, drained him. He threw his head back as the climax shook him to the core, taking everything from him.

He laced their fingers together as another explosion went off within him. His final thought before exhaustion claimed him was that he didn't think he could ever let her go.

Seven

Wesley blinked at the sunlight that poured brightly through the window.

The storm was over.

He glanced around the unfamiliar bedroom seeing the flowers, the large fluffy pillows and stuffed animals. Soft colors of mauve and light gray mingled with bold splashes of black. The room's decor was accentuated with a floral print on the valances over the window and in the matching bedspread.

He glanced at the empty spot next to him and frowned; he was surprised that Jasmine could even walk this morning after their activities of the night before. One climax had led to another and then another and pretty soon, he'd lost count.

Each time they had reach the pinnacles of ecstasy together, it had been better than before. Being inside her and hearing her cry out his name had truly been a unique experience in more ways than one. He had never taken part in anything so breathtakingly beautiful and passionate in his entire life.

He slipped out of the bed when he heard her moving around in the kitchen and smelled the aroma of coffee. He couldn't wait to see her. He hoped that she didn't have any regrets. Pulling on his jeans, he snapped them up as he heard her phone rang. He walked out of the bedroom after the fourth ring and realized she had no intentions of answering it. He was nearly in the kitchen when he heard the answering machine pick up the message.

"Jasmine, this is Alyssa and I know you're home so don't pretend otherwise. I don't know if you plan to attend the huge benefit ball given by the hospital in two weeks, but I've decided to let you know that Paul Sanders will be my date that night. We ran into each other this past week and renewed our friendship, if you know what I mean." There was a snicker in her voice when she added, "I thought I would prepare you. Goodbye."

Wesley frowned. He remembered she had said that Paul Sanders had been the man she had once planned to marry. He stepped into the kitchen and his gaze immediately went to her. She was wearing a short robe and was standing at the window with her back to him.

Her head was lowered, as if her stepsister's words were more than she cared to deal with at the moment. He wondered if he should return to the bedroom and pretend he hadn't heard the recording, then decided not to. If he wanted to find out what was driving Jasmine then he needed to know everything about her.

Crossing the room he walked up behind her. He reached out and pulled her back against him and wrapped his arms around her, needing to touch her, to be close to her.

"The bed was empty," he whispered softly against her ear. He slowly turned her around so he could look at her. "I missed you." Brushing his mouth against hers.

When he lifted his mouth, he eyed her closely and saw heat flood her cheeks and understood why. She had been a sensual delight in his arms last night and now she was not sure how to act the morning after.

"I needed to take a bath and soak a while," she said softly.

He reached out and touched her cheek, knowing her body had to be tender. "I didn't mean to make love to you so many times."

"Yeah, but I asked for it," she responded truthfully. "And I have no regrets."

Wesley released a deep sigh, grateful to hear that because he had no regrets, either. He glanced around the kitchen. She had set out eggs and bacon to cook. "If you prefer I can take you out to breakfast."

She chuckled. "No, that's okay. I enjoy cooking. It won't take but a minute to throw something together."

He nodded. "What are your plans today?"

She shrugged. "Saturdays are usually my lazy days. Once in a while I'll go into the office if I'm working on a story, but today I'd planned to stay in and relax."

"How would you like spending the day with me? I

have to go to Charleston to make a few deliveries and return later tonight. I'd love the company.''

Jasmine opened her mouth to refuse his invitation but for some reason she couldn't. She wasn't ready for her time with him to end just yet. She met Wesley's gaze. She would go to Charleston with him but needed to make sure that he had a clear understanding about something. ''Will this be a date?''

He lifted a brow. ''Why?''

''Because I don't date. I told you that before.''

He nodded. Yes, she had. He also remembered the reason she had given him as to why she didn't date. ''You slept with me last night,'' he decided to remind her. Most women didn't sleep with men they didn't date unless it was just a one-night stand. And hell would freeze over before he would let that happen.

Although he dated a lot of women, he didn't sleep with just anyone. He was known to have very discriminating taste when it came to women and with Jasmine having been a virgin, he knew she didn't sleep around either. The fact that he had been the first man she had slept with changed everything.

''Yes, but it wasn't a date.''

He smiled down at her, his eyes curious. ''In your mind, what constitutes a date?''

She shrugged again. ''A couple going out and doing things together, going places together on a constant basis, like dinner, to the movies, concerts—things like that. Last night was our first and our last time sleeping together. Nothing has changed, Wesley. I'm still the reporter you don't like.''

She was wrong; everything had changed. She might

be a reporter he didn't like but she was also a woman he desired. And she was wrong about last night being the last time they would sleep together. He definitely had plans to make love to her again.

"I liked you well enough last night. In fact I liked you a whole hell of a lot. And do you know what I liked most?" he asked her.

She held his gaze for a long, uncertain moment before asking in a whispered voice. "What?"

"I especially like the way you call my name when you come apart while I'm making love to you."

"Wesley, you can't—"

He didn't give her a chance to finish what she was about to say. He reached down and swung her into his arms and captured her mouth in a kiss. His mind was made up. He wanted her and intended to have her.

He made his way back toward her bedroom. It would be a while before he made love to her the traditional way since her body was still sore, but he knew another way he could make love to her and it was a way that she had already enjoyed. Before the day was over, she would remember his every touch.

The moment Jasmine walked into Wesley's spacious two-story home she was captivated. Beautiful polished hardwood floors greeted her when she stepped into the foyer. The most gorgeous chandelier she'd ever seen hung overhead. The crystals dripping from the chandelier actually looked like diamonds and she had to blink to make sure they weren't.

A spiral staircase loomed ahead and Jasmine could imagine all the grand parties that had been given in the older home, which appeared to have been built in the eighteen hundreds. But what took Jasmine's breath away more than anything was the beautiful view of the Savannah River from almost every room in the house.

He had furnished the house with period furnishings. Each piece made the house retain its original splendor and made her feel like she was taking a step back in time. Just from glancing around, she could tell he enjoyed having nice things. So did she.

After touring the downstairs, they walked up the stairs to the second floor. "You have an office both upstairs and downstairs?" she asked, after taking a glance at another room with a computer, bookcase and a desk.

"Yes. I do a lot of work at home although my business has office space on the river front. Besides my bedroom, there are two additional bedrooms up here that have their own baths. I have a master bath in my bedroom. I decided to put off decorating the additional bedrooms for now since there wasn't an urgent need to do so. In fact I use one of them for storage."

When they entered his bedroom she was in awe and couldn't help but stare shamelessly at his huge bed while something stirred deep within her. She tried averting her attention from his bed to the other impressive furnishings in the room but found that she couldn't. She could see herself in that bed with him making love. She glanced up and met his gaze and the look in his eyes indicated that he could imagine the same thing.

"Let me show you the master bath," he said

hoarsely, leading her into an area off from the bedroom. His bathroom was as large as one of the bedrooms downstairs and had a huge Jacuzzi tub, as well
as a large shower. Another image filled her mind; one
of them taking a bath together.

She turned to Wesley. "Your home is beautiful."

Wesley reached out and touched her chin with his
fingers. It pleased him that she liked his home and
without thinking twice about it, he leaned down and
gently kissed her lips.

The kiss was slow and soul deep. Jasmine's heart
lurched at his tenderness.

Moments later she experienced a tinge of regret
when he pulled his mouth back to end the kiss. "I
guess we better get going," he whispered against her
still-moist lips.

She nodded. "Yes, I guess we'd better."

As they walked down the stairs together, she
thought about how much she enjoyed the kisses they
shared. Somehow Wesley had the ability to elevate a
simple kiss to a sensuous art form.

They walked through his kitchen with the spotless
appliances, beautiful tiled counters and floors, and oak
cabinets to his four-car garage. In addition to the Mercedes and Explorer and Corvette that she'd known he
owned, a huge Harley Davidson motorcycle was also
parked in one of the garage spaces.

She glanced up at him when he opened the door to
the Explorer for her. "You like riding your motorcycle?"

He smiled and even before he gave her an answer,
she knew that he did. "Yes, occasionally I enjoy hit-

ting the open road. Sometimes there's nothing like the feel of wind in your face."

After making sure her seat belt was secure, he closed the door and walked around to the front of the vehicle to get into the driver's side. Jasmine peered over her shoulder into the back seat of the SUV and saw all the books stocked on the seat. "You're delivering books?" she asked in surprise.

He glanced over at her as he started the engine. "Yes. A friend of mine from college runs the boys' club in Charleston. I usually check with him periodically to see what items he may need since funding for the club has been drastically cut over the years. When I talked to him last week he indicated they were trying to steer the boys away from playing video games and focus their free time on reading, so I offered to buy a few books."

Jasmine nodded. Wesley had bought more than a few. There were over a hundred books in his Explorer. She couldn't help but think about the Wesley Brooks she was getting to know. Her father had always said that a person's deeds reflected their true inner self and part of her couldn't help wondering how many people, other than the Danforths, had the opportunity to see this side of Wesley.

The drive from Savannah to Charleston was pleasant. A wave of sadness touched her when Wesley opened himself up and told her about his childhood, that period of time when he'd been moved from foster home to foster home. What he'd gone through made what she'd experienced with Evelyn and her stepsisters look like nothing. At least she had always known she'd had the love of her father and had been fortunate to have had her mother's love for a while. But Wesley hadn't known what family was until the Danforths had come into his life. Now she understood his love and loyalty for them.

"Here we are," he said, bringing the vehicle to a stop in front of a huge building. "Luke works hard to keep the boys off the street and channel their energy into worthwhile projects."

"Luke?"

"Yes, Luke Murdock."

Jasmine blinked. "Luke Murdock? *The* Luke Murdock?"

Wesley smiled. "Yes, the Luke Murdock." Most people had heard about the kid from the small town in Blakely, Georgia, who had later played football at Georgia Tech and had gone on to play professionally, becoming one of the most noted quarterbacks in the history of the NFL before an injury ended his football career a few years ago.

"And the two of you went to college together?" Jasmine asked, still in shock that she was about to meet Luke Murdock.

"Yes, we used to play ball together at GT." Wesley sighed deeply. What he wasn't ready to share with Jasmine was how because of Caroline Perry's article, he had gotten kicked off the football team and shunned by the majority of his teammates. Of all the guys on the team, Luke had been one of the few who had stuck by him through the entire ordeal, giving him support and friendship, and even going so far as to ask their coach not to take him off the team. However, the coach had stuck to his decision by saying the information Wesley had given Caroline had been too damaging and had cast a bad light on the entire team.

Not wanting to think about that part of his past any longer, Wesley glanced over at Jasmine and thought about the time they had spent together. A sensuous shiver made a path up his spine when he thought about making love to her, thrusting inside of her, the way her fingernails dug deep into his shoulder blades, branding him. Everything about her wanted to make him reach out and touch her. The woman was simply distracting.

Even now he enjoyed being in her presence and was glad she had agreed to come to Charleston with him. "When we're through here, I'd like to rent a sailboat and have lunch on the Charleston Harbor. Would you like that?"

Tossing her head to look at him, her braids settled in a way that framed her face. When she tilted her head and met his gaze, he felt as if he'd been punched in the stomach. "Yes, I'd like that, Wesley."

Before renting a boat, Wesley and Jasmine visited Charleston's premiere shopping district on King Street. Since Ronnie's birthday was in a few weeks, Jasmine thought now would be a good time to pick out a gift for her friend. Then they enjoyed a carriage ride on East Battery, a section of town located on the harbor. The oleanders along East Battery were in full bloom and they were a delight to the senses.

After picking up a packed lunch at a restaurant that Luke had recommended, they walked hand in hand around Waterfront Park, basking in the beauty of their surroundings. Jasmine had really liked Luke and could see why he and Wesley were good friends. Both were fiercely loyal to the people they considered friends, and from the look on Luke's face she could tell he had appreciated the books Wesley had delivered to him.

"Do you know how to operate a sailboat, Jasmine?"

Wesley's question interrupted her thoughts and she glanced up at him. "No. If you were depending on me being your backup then you're out of luck."

Wesley grinned. "No, I was just wondering how anyone who has lived in Savannah for as long as you have hadn't been interested enough to find out. I can't imagine not going out on the water at least once a week. That's the beauty of living in Savannah, even during the winter months, you can enjoy the river."

Jasmine nodded. "Do you own a boat?"

"Yes, I have a sailboat, as well as a cabin cruiser that Jake and I own together."

Sharing lunch with Wesley on the Charleston Harbor was a wonderful experience, Jasmine thought as she watched him expertly handle the sailboat. At one point after having a conversation about several movies they had seen, they had fallen into silence. She had glanced up to find him watching her intently like she was a puzzle he was trying to piece together. It didn't bother her that he was seeing another side of her because she was seeing another side of him, as well. There was work and then there was play and she was enjoying being able to relax in his presence. They hadn't mentioned anything about Abraham Danforth and the campaign since Wesley had shown up at her place for dinner last night.

Later that afternoon when they had returned to Savannah and Wesley walked her to the door, she invited him in. As soon as the door was closed behind them he gathered her into his arms and kissed her and she had to lock her knees to keep them from buckling under her.

His kiss sharpened her senses and filled her with an intense need to return it with all the longing she felt. She regretted the moment their lips parted and he took a step back.

"Thanks for going to Charleston with me today," he said huskily while his gaze zeroed in on her lips.

"Thanks for inviting me to go. I had fun."

"So did I. What are you doing tomorrow?"

"Attending church service and having dinner at my father's. It's a weekly ritual and because of his schedule, sometimes it's the only time the two of us can spend together."

He nodded. "And after dinner?"

"Ronnie and I are going to see several movies. A co-worker of ours who reviews movies is out of town this weekend and asked if we would do so in his absence and we told him that we would." A smile touched her lips. "But I'm sure that you and I will be running into each other sometime this week, right?" She knew he had every intention of continuing to follow her around. The thought of him doing so no longer bothered her.

He grinned. "Right. We'll definitely run into each other this week."

After kissing her again, he opened the door and left.

"So what did you do yesterday? I tried calling you a few times and couldn't get you."

Jasmine glanced up at Ronnie from across the table. They had taken a break in between movies to grab another soda and more popcorn. She wondered what her best friend would say if she knew that she had spent Friday night with Wesley and then all day Saturday in Charleston with him, as well. She was not ready to let anyone else in on what was going on between them. She wanted to savor the secret a while longer, especially since Ronnie knew she had considered Wesley her enemy just few weeks ago.

"I did all sorts of things," Jasmine said, thinking that really wasn't a lie. She met Ronnie's gaze. "What about you? What did you do?"

Ronnie smiled. "Dan and I drove down to Amelia Island and spent the entire day on the beach. It was fun. I'm still trying to get him to make me into a naughty girl but he won't budge."

Jasmine bit her lip to keep from grinning. Dan and Ronnie had been dating for almost six months and still they hadn't slept together. He didn't want them to rush into anything and no matter what Ronnie did or said, he hadn't changed his mind. "I wouldn't give up if I were you. Just keep trying, he's going to surrender sooner or later."

Ronnie chuckled. "I hope it's sooner than later. Trust me, I intend to keep tempting him. In fact, how would you like going shopping with me tomorrow? I want to buy something sexy that's guaranteed to get his attention.''

Jasmine laughed. "It shouldn't be hard finding such an item.''

Ronnie joined her in laughter. "I'm counting on it.'' After their laughter subsided, Ronnie asked. "So how are things going with that Danforth assignment? Any new developments?''

Jasmine shook her head. The last time she'd been out to Crofthaven had been for the press conference where Abraham had revealed the coroner's report regarding the cause of death. "No, things have been pretty quiet. I really don't expect things to start heating up until the election gets into full swing.''

"And what about Wesley Brooks?''

Jasmine took a sip of her drink, deciding not to meet Ronnie's gaze and asked. "What about him?''

"Is he still following you around?''

Jasmine felt a thickness in her throat. Not only was he following her around, he had parked himself real snug in her bed a few nights ago. "Yes, he's still following me around.''

"And you're handling it okay?''

If only you knew just how well I'm handling it. "Yes, I'm handling it fine. I'm used to it now.''

Ronnie nodded as she checked her watch. "It's almost time for the next movie to start. Oh, by the way, I'm covering that big social event sponsored by the hospital in a few weeks. I noticed your father is one of the doctors being honored. Are you going?''

"Yes, although I got a call from Alyssa the other day to let me know that she's going with Paul."

Ronnie frowned. "Paul Sanders?" At Jasmine's nod Ronnie's frown deepened. "When are they going to let up and get a life? I can't believe after what happened she would do something like that."

Jasmine shook her head. "You and Alyssa have different values and standards. You would never have done what she did. I'm sure Paul being Alyssa's date will have Dad wondering what's going on."

Ronnie nodded. "You never told your father why the two of you broke up and about Evelyn's part in it? If he knew, Evelyn, Mallory and Alyssa would be history."

"Yes, but then where would they go?"

"Who gives a royal flip? If I were you I wouldn't give a damn. Besides, your father would be better off without them. I'm sure his bank account definitely would be."

Jasmine couldn't disagree with that last comment. "I still can't do that no matter how mean and hateful they are."

"Well, as far as I'm concerned Evelyn is a real witch. She makes Cinderella's stepmother look like an angel."

Jasmine only nodded. She had learned a long time ago not to let her stepmother and stepsisters get to her.

"What time do you want to go shopping tomorrow?"

"Right after work." A thought then crossed Ronnie's mind. "You don't think Wesley Brooks will follow us, do you?"

Jasmine shrugged. "Probably not. Why?"

"Just curious, especially since we plan on visiting stores that sell sexy lingerie. I don't want him getting any ideas about you."

Jasmine smiled. After Friday night, Wesley probably had gotten plenty of ideas about her.

Eight

He couldn't get Jasmine off his mind.

Even a week later while having dinner with Harold and Miranda at their home along with Jake, Larissa and their son, Peter, Wesley was flooded with memories. He continued to shadow Jasmine but now it was with an entirely new intent. He liked seeing her and watching her.

Trying to give her time to adjust to the turn their relationship had taken, he hadn't been over to her place since dropping her off Saturday night. But he'd seen her every day. He remembered how they had gone sailing on the Charleston Harbor and sat side by side sharing lunch. Even then, he had fought the urge to take her in his arms and make love to her right then and there.

"Are you all right, Wesley?"

Wesley quickly raised his gaze to the end of the table at the sound of Miranda Danforth's soft voice. She was looking at him with concern and so was everyone else at the table. He suddenly realized why. She had asked him a question a while ago and he had yet to answer.

"Yes, I'm fine," he answered smiling, focusing on the woman with the warm blue eyes who had always been there for him after he'd come to live with her and Harold in this huge house. From the moment they had invited him into their home, not only as their son's best friend, but also as a member of their family, an unofficially adopted son, they had occupied a special place in his heart. All the Danforths had.

"She asked if you've been dating anyone special lately," Harold Danforth chuckled, repeating his wife's question. His eyebrows were heavy over kind blue eyes. "Now that Jake's married off, she's determined to see what she can do about you since it seems that Toby and Imogene are lost causes."

Wesley smiled. Tobias, whom everyone fondly called Toby, was Harold and Miranda's divorced twenty-nine-year-old son who lived in Wyoming. Everyone knew that like Ian, Toby had no plans to ever remarry. And Imogene was married to her career. Not surprising to anyone, she had called earlier to say she would miss dinner because she was on the run and was trying to squeeze in a late appointment with a potential client.

"Well, Wesley, are you dating?"

Wesley's smile widened at Miranda's question. He remembered when he and Jake had lived at home, Miranda would wait for them after their dates to find out how things had gone. Of course he and Jake had never told her *everything*. But just the thought that she had cared enough to ask had meant a lot to him and he'd never considered it as meddling like Jake often had.

He glanced quickly across the table and met Jake's smile and knew his best friend thought his mother was meddling now. "No, I'm not dating but I am seeing someone," he finally answered.

He saw the bemused frown settle on Miranda's brow. He understood her confusion since the situation confused him, too. However, Jasmine was determined not to "date" him. As far as he was concerned, she could call it what she liked as long as he got to see her and be with her.

"Will we get a chance to meet her?" Jake asked grinning.

Wesley shot his best friend a warning glance. Jake was the only one at the table who knew the woman he was seeing was Jasmine Carmody and just how deep their relationship had gotten. Although none of them other than Jake and Larissa had met Jasmine, everyone knew her name and knew her to be the persistent reporter hounding the Danforths. He smiled when he thought of what everyone's reaction would be when he brought her to dinner, which was something he planned to do when she realized that he intended to remain a part of her life for a while.

"I'll bring her around soon. Right now she's rather shy." He ignored the sound of Jake nearly choking on his wine. "But, her shyness is something that I'm working on."

Miranda smiled. "Good, and we look forward to meeting her."

Wesley returned her smile. He looked forward to introducing Jasmine to the people that he cared about. Then she would see that the Danforths were warm, caring people who had nothing to hide.

Wesley stood under Jasmine's porch light as she opened the door. Usually he would follow her home from her last interview then go to his own place. He had wanted to give her time to adjust to how things were between them. In addition, she had been a virgin and he had wanted to be considerate and give her body time to recover from last Friday night. So he had waited out a week, but now he wanted her again.

He met her gaze, staring into the darkness of her brown eyes.

Wesley watched her swallow. He noticed her breathing had quickened and the way she nibbled on her bottom lip. She had gotten his message loud and clear. She stepped back and without hesitating, he walked into the house and quickly closed the door behind him.

Driven by a need to show her how much he wanted her, he lowered his head and captured her mouth in his.

With a surrendering sigh, Jasmine opened her mouth to his. When he took her tongue and ensnared it with his, pleasure points went off all through her body. She forgot everything, except for how he was making her feel.

He had never kissed her like this before, with such

intensity and fervor—absolute wildness. But tonight it seemed that something was driving him, and whatever it was, she was too powerless to deny him whatever he wanted.

Although she didn't understand what was spurring him on, she wanted it. She needed to be enveloped in him; wrapped tight in his strength, encased in his love....

The thought burst her sensual bubble.

Get real, Jasmine. A few weeks ago the man caught you going through his garbage. Do you really think he's fallen for you just because you slept together? Face it. This is lust and not love. This is a matter of being hot and not a matter of the heart.

But, as Wesley lowered her to the carpeted floor and she felt his impatient fingers lifting her skirt, she didn't care what it was. At the moment all she desired the most was a chance to lose herself in him and to be a part of him. She released a hungry sigh from deep within her throat as he eased her panties off, closed her eyes and took pleasure in what he was doing to her.

Wesley heard the sensual sound emitting from Jasmine's throat and felt the quick pounding of his heart. He pulled his mouth from hers and leaned back and looked down at her. She was gorgeous, laying on the carpet with her skirt to her waist and naked below.

A lump formed in his throat. He became mesmerized as he gazed upon her. She reopened her eyes and saw her confusion as he continued to stare at her. Nervously, she made a move to cover herself with her hands.

He reached out and stopped her. "No, I love looking at you," he said huskily, while slowly unzipping his pants.

"You make me crazy, Jasmine," he said, giving her a half smile and thinking he'd never been this aroused before, to the point that the only thing that mattered was getting inside of a woman. There was no logic to what he was thinking or to what he was doing.

"And *that*," he said, indicating the part of her she had tried shielding from his view, "makes me delirious with need."

Pulling out his wallet, he removed a foil-wrapped condom and proceeded to protect them both, knowing that she was watching his every move.

He went to her and began stroking her, glorying in her dampness, in her scent and the sounds she began making.

A low growl escaped his throat when he eased his body over hers and slowly entered her. When he felt her body pulse around him, her feminine muscles tightening, he completely lost it and thrust within her hard and deep. He leaned down and kissed her with an intensity that made her body shiver. He released her lips and she moaned out his name.

Whatever control he had suddenly broke and he made love with her like a madman enjoying what would be his last sexual encounter with the woman who meant everything to him.

That thought had him scared straight but it was too late. The dye had been cast and he couldn't fight what he was feeling any longer. When he felt her body explode around him and heard her cry out, he pushed into her one last time glorying in the explosion that rocked his body, as well as hers.

And at that moment, Wesley knew what it felt to be out of control but totally in sync with a woman. He knew the difference between having sex and making love. He was drowning in ecstasy of the richest and most profound kind, and he knew from this night forward his life would never be the same.

A short while later, Wesley was still stretched out on the carpet with Jasmine in his arms. He looked down at her and saw her lashes flutter open slowly, trying to catch her breath the same way he was trying to catch his. He suddenly found the strength to whisper. "I wanted you so much."

He waited for her to speak, but when she did, her words took him by surprise. "I thought just the opposite. After following me home, I thought you would leave without coming in like you did all week," she said in a quiet tone of voice.

He reached out and caressed her cheek. "Only because I wanted to give you a chance to get used to the idea of us, as well as to give your body time to adjust," he said softly.

She nodded knowing what he'd said was true and appreciated his thoughtfulness.

"Give me a second and I'll be back," he said.

Jasmine watched as he stood and walked off in the direction of her bathroom. She sat up, put her panties back on and pulled down her skirt, not believing they had actually made love on the floor, just a few feet from her front door.

Wesley returned to see Jasmine sitting in the same spot where he'd left her. The first thing he noticed was that she had her clothes back on straight and a part of him regretted that since he so much enjoyed seeing them in disarray or completely off.

Walking over to her, he crouched down in front of her and took her hand in his. Lifting her hand to his lips he kissed her fingers gently. "Are you ready to talk?"

She frowned, deepening the lines between her brows. "About what?"

"About us and dating," he told her, deciding to sit beside her on the carpeted floor. He kept her hand in his. "I want you to consider it. In fact I want you to be my date at the benefit dinner the hospital is giving next week."

She shook her head and nervously bit her bottom lip. "Wesley, I don't think that's a good idea."

"Why, because your ex-fiancé will be there?"

Jasmine lifted a brow, wondering how he knew then remembered Alyssa's phone call last Saturday morning. Evidently he had heard her stepsister's message.

"That's not it at all. Paul means nothing to me."

"Then why are you letting your stepmother and stepsisters dictate your social life?"

"I'm not. I just don't want to cause problems. If Dad knew what was going on, he would give Evelyn and her daughters their walking papers so fast it would make their heads spin."

"Then let him," Wesley said roughly.

She shook her head. "I can't do that, Wesley. Evelyn and my father have been married for almost ten years. She depends on his money, so do Alyssa and Mallory. They wouldn't know what to do if they had to fend for themselves."

"Then maybe it's time they found out," he said, his tone lacking sympathy of any kind. "How can your father not know what's going on when you eat dinner with them every Sunday?"

"Yes, but with everything that he's involved with at the hospital, he's a very busy man and doesn't know how bad my relationship with Evelyn, Mallory and Alyssa really is. Whenever he's around they're on their best behavior."

Wesley shook his head as he pulled himself to his feet and brought Jasmine up with him. "I know for a fact that you aren't someone who doesn't fight back when boxed in a corner," he said remembering that night they had squared off at the coffeehouse.

"Don't let their actions control you."

"I won't."

He lifted her chin up with his finger to meet his gaze. "Good. That means I will be your date that night, all right?"

Jasmine knew to argue about it would be useless. He was proving to be as stubborn as she was about certain things. "All right."

He gently pulled her into his arms, drawing her close. Jasmine felt the tension seep out of her and she drew comfort from the strong arms around her.

Wesley took a quick glance at the clock on Jasmine's nightstand the moment he heard his cell phone go off. Pushing himself up in bed he reached over and grabbed it off the nightstand where he had placed it earlier. "Hello," he said in a deep, sleepy voice. He felt Jasmine stirring beside him.

"Wes, this is Jake. I'm glad you had your cell phone on at this hour. I just got a call from Ian. There's been an explosion at the Danforth and Danforth waterfront office. Luckily no one was hurt. I'm contacting the family to let them know so they can get here immediately. In a few minutes the place will be swarming with police and reporters."

Wesley's brain was filled with urgent questions. But he knew that now was not the time to ask. He'd get the answers to all his questions once he got to the waterfront. "I'm on my way," he said before ending the call and hanging up the phone.

"Something wrong, Wes?"

He turned to Jasmine. Tonight he had kissed her until she'd consented to call him Wes instead of Wesley. "Yes, that was Jake. There's been an explosion at the Danforth and Danforth waterfront office."

"An explosion?" she asked anxiously as her heart skipped a beat. "Was anyone hurt?"

He stood and quickly began putting on his clothes. "No, no one was hurt and I didn't get the chance to ask how bad things were. Jake was too busy trying to reach other family members. I told him I was on my way."

Jasmine slipped out of the bed. "I'm going with you," she said and met his gaze when he stopped stuffing his shirt into his pants. Her heart missed another beat and she said softly, "I'm a reporter, Wes, but I'm sure the newspaper will have someone there covering the story. Tonight I'll be there as your friend. You're going to have to trust me.''

For a long moment he gazed into her eyes, not wanting to remember how trusting Caroline had gotten him burned. But something deep within him wanted to trust Jasmine. "All right, I trust you, Jasmine.''

An hour later Jasmine pinched her nose against the sting of the smoke still in the air. When they arrived at the waterfront they'd found the place in chaos, swarming with firemen, policemen, reporters and members of the Danforth family. Ian had been busy giving the investigating detective what information he had and several police officers and firemen were doing a thorough job of searching through the debris in an attempt to discover the cause of the explosion. Luckily the damage had not been extensive.

Jasmine glanced around. It seemed that the entire second generation of Danforths had crowded into the main office where the detective was asking questions. No one in the family had questioned her right to be there as she stood next to Wes. They had seen them arrive together and had probably drawn their own conclusions about their connection—especially since it was so early in the morning.

"You're sure you don't have any enemies, business or otherwise, that you can think of Mr. Danforth?'' the detective asked, giving Ian a level stare.

Ian returned the man's scrutiny with a stare of his own. "That's right. As far as I know I don't have any enemies, Detective. None of the Danforths do.''

After a long moment, the detective nodded. "If you happen to think of anything else that can help us, here's my card," he said. "Give me a call. In the meantime, I plan to hang around and talk to the officers and firemen to see what other information they may have." Everyone watched as the detective walked out.

Hours later almost everyone had left except for Ian, Reid, Wes, Jake and Marcus. Adam Danforth was out of town. So were Kim and her husband Zack.

"I'm glad no one was hurt," Marcus Danforth said to the occupants left in the room. He was Abraham's youngest son. Harvard educated, he was an attorney for Danforth and Danforth.

Jasmine sat in Ian's office while the five men stood around Ian's desk and talked openly in front of her. They knew her profession and they also knew about her past efforts in trying to dig information up on their family, yet they trusted Wes. If he felt she was not a threat then so would they.

"Why didn't you tell that detective about Sonny Hernandez and your suspicions, Ian?" Jake asked looking over at his cousin.

Wes raised a brow. "Who's Sonny Hernandez?"

Ian raked a hand down his tired face before he answered. "The guy's real name is Jamie Hernandez, but he goes by Sonny. He's a coffee supplier who came to me months ago with a deal that I turned down."

Marcus Danforth crossed his arms over his chest and leaned against the desk. "What sort of deal?"

"I don't think I want to know," Reid said, chiming in before Ian had a chance to answer Marcus's question.

"The man wanted me to consider doing business

with certain coffee suppliers and I turned him down. I didn't feel good about what he proposed because I know that a few of the suppliers he named are disreputable,'' Ian said.

"And you think this Sonny person may have something to do with tonight's explosion?'' Wes asked in an angry voice.

"Hell, I don't know,'' Ian said. "The entire proposal that Hernandez offered sounded rather shady and he got rather pissed that I didn't see things his way.''

"Pissed enough to do something like this?'' Jake asked angrily.

"Yes, especially if he's a front for some bigger operation,'' Ian replied. "I didn't want to mention him to the police until I can get more information about him.''

For the longest moment the room got quiet, and then Ian met Wesley's gaze in silent acknowledgement. Ian then shifted his gaze to glance to Jasmine. "Is there any way you can help us in finding out whether he's part of a bigger operation?''

Jasmine swallowed. She had been tempted to offer her services but wasn't sure of her place. But in asking for her help, Ian was letting her know that he trusted her, too.

"Yes, that's something I can find out,'' she said softly. "If Sonny Hernandez is using his business as a front for some organized crime cartel, then I'll be able to find that out. I have some contacts at the police station and I can discreetly find out what you want to know.''

Ian nodded. "All right and thanks.''

Instead of taking her back home, Wesley took Jasmine to his place since he lived closer. It was nearly daybreak and both were too tense and wired to sleep. They sat at the kitchen table drinking cups of coffee.

"What do you think it will mean if Hernandez is involved in some kind of money-laundering scheme for organized crime?"

"I just hope he isn't," Jasmine said after taking a sip of coffee. "Men like that are ruthless and will do just about anything to get what they want."

Wesley nodded. "How soon do you think you can find out anything?"

"If I can touch base with my contact tomorrow, then I'll have the information in a few days," she replied.

Wesley sighed deeply. "I wonder if any of this has to do with those threatening e-mails Abraham received."

Jasmine lifted a brow. "What threatening e-mails?"

Wesley met her gaze and didn't say anything for a while. She knew he was trying to make a decision about something—how much he felt he could tell her. Earlier that night he had said he trusted her and now he was faced with proving just how much.

She released the breath she wasn't aware she'd been holding when he began talking, telling her about the three e-mails Abraham had received and the virus one of them had carried. "Is he still getting them?" she asked. She couldn't help but admire the Danforths' ability to keep the threats from leaking to the media.

"As far as I know he's not."

Jasmine nodded. "What is Abraham doing about it

if he hasn't gone to the police? I hope he took those threats seriously.''

Wesley took another sip of his coffee. ''He did and has hired a security specialist by the name of Michael Whittaker to work on the case. It's my understanding that Whittaker is good at what he does.''

Jasmine nodded again and like Wesley, began wondering if the incidents were related. ''I'll find out as much as I can, Wesley.''

''Thanks, and we appreciate it.''

It didn't take Jasmine long to ask the right questions of the right person to get the information she needed. Two days later she met with Wes, Ian, Reid, Marcus and Jake again.

She placed a sealed report in Ian's hand. ''It's all there, viable information that Hernandez's company is really a front for a cartel money-laundering operation.''

Ignoring Reid's long whistle she continued. ''You did the right thing by turning down his deal, Ian. The man is connected to a drug cartel and wants to use certain coffee bean suppliers as part of their smuggling operations.''

''Yes, but if he's responsible for the explosion, look how he retaliated,'' Jake said angrily. ''Can't we take that report to the police and demand that they do something?''

Jasmine shook her head. ''No, especially since we can't prove Hernandez is responsible for the explosion. It would be sheer speculation on our part.''

''So what am I supposed to do? Sit around for them to make their next move?'' Ian asked angrily.

"No," Jasmine said, touching Ian's arm to calm his anger. "Don't let them get to you. The explosion is their way of letting you know they mean business and want you to begin seeing things their way. It's my guess that they'll sit still for a while and give you time to absorb what they've done so the next time they approach you, you'll agree to do business with them."

"When hell freezes over," Ian snarled.

Jasmine smiled. Ian's anger reminded her so much of Wesley's. It was uncanny how the five men in the room had varied similarities. "Well, at least with that report you know what you're up against."

"Jasmine's right," Marcus decided to add. "Legally, our hands are tied unless we have concrete proof that Hernandez is responsible."

When the meeting ended, Wesley and Jasmine were walking back toward his car. He gently snagged her arm, pulled her in a darkened area of the parking lot and covered her mouth in a deep, drugging kiss.

"Thank you," he said, ending the kiss moments later. His warm breath whispered across her face like a sensual caress.

She smiled. "You are very welcome." She then leaned up on tiptoes and covered his mouth with hers, needing to taste him again.

Nine

Jasmine released a nervous sigh when she walked into the grand ballroom of the Savannah Hyatt Regency Riverfront Hotel alone. Drawing in a calming breath, she smiled when she remembered the valet attendant's compliment on how she looked. The young man had blushed profusely and told her she looked like a princess before he'd taken her car keys.

She had gotten a call from Wesley yesterday. He had left Savannah for a business trip to Dallas three days ago and was supposed to have returned yesterday, but a snag in a business deal had kept him in Dallas another day. He wouldn't arrive back in Savannah until tomorrow morning. She had decided to come to the ball without a date which she would have done anyway had Wesley not insisted on coming with her.

Jasmine glanced around the room, taking in the well-dressed, affluent people in their expensive suits and gowns. She didn't see Evelyn and her stepsisters anywhere, but she did see her father standing with a group of men. He saw her the same moment she saw him and his face split into a huge smile. She walked over to him and gave him a huge hug.

"Jasmine, I'm so glad you came, sweetheart," her father said, smiling brightly.

"I would not have missed it, Dad," she said truthfully.

She then turned as he introduced her to the other men standing with him. "This beautiful, young lady here is my daughter Jasmine."

One of the men, who looked to be about thirty-five and whom her father had introduced as Dr. Simon Duncan, smiled appreciatively at her. "I watched her enter, Dr. Carmody, and wondered who she was. I wasn't aware you had a third daughter."

Dr. James Carmody beamed. "Yes, Jasmine is my daughter from my first marriage. Alyssa and Mallory are my stepdaughters."

The man nodded and met Jasmine's gaze. "I hope you'll save a dance for me later, Ms. Carmody."

Jasmine smiled. "I'll most definitely do that, Dr. Duncan."

Moments later Jasmine left her father's side to go to the buffet table to get something to eat. "I see that you're here without a date, which doesn't surprise me. Maybe you should talk to Mallory and Alyssa about the proper techniques in getting a man," a voice sneered in her ear.

Without turning around she knew whom the voice

belonged to. "Thanks for the advice but I like doing things my way, Evelyn."

The smile that touched her stepmother's lips didn't reflect in her eyes. "Yes, but your way isn't producing results." After taking a sip of wine, Evelyn continued by saying, "I happened to notice you were talking to Dr. Duncan a few moments ago. Don't get any ideas about him because Mallory already has him pegged."

Evelyn then glanced around. "Alyssa as you know is here with Paul, although her true interest lies elsewhere. She's smitten with someone who hasn't made an appearance yet." A smile then touched her lips. "I spoke too soon. It seems he has arrived."

Jasmine glanced over her shoulder and a lump formed in her throat when she saw Wesley enter the room. She shook her head in shock. First at seeing him and then at what Evelyn had said. Had she heard her stepmother correctly? Did Alyssa have designs on Wes? This was news to her and evidently it wasn't something Wesley was aware of, either.

Jasmine, like most of every other female in the room, watched as he snagged a glass of wine from the tray of a passing waiter and took a sip. He looked like he was born to wear a tuxedo. He had the ability to take your breath away just looking at him. He'd obviously been able to shorten his meeting and return home for tonight's function after all.

"You probably don't know him but that's Wesley Brooks and he's the biggest catch in the city. Every time he appears at one of these functions, I make sure either Mallory or Alyssa gets in his face," Evelyn whispered to her. "The Danforths consider him a part of their family. He's definitely caught Alyssa's interest and she won't be satisfied until she has him."

Jasmine's cheek twitched in anger and her hold on the plate tightened. She hated to disappoint Alyssa if that's what she thought, and then wondered what Evelyn would say if she knew that Wesley was to have been her date tonight.

She watched as he glanced around. Suddenly, he caught her gaze. He smiled and was about to head over in her direction when Harold and Miranda Danforth stopped him for a conversation.

"I think he was about to come this way," Evelyn whispered. "I wonder if he remembers me from another function and wants to inquire about Alyssa."

Jasmine shook her head. It was sad that her stepmother thought the world revolved around her and her daughters. She would soon find out that wasn't the case.

She inhaled deeply and decided to make herself scarce until she could talk to Wesley alone, to let him know about Alyssa. Her stepsister was like a spoiled brat and could be a real bitch if things didn't go the way she wanted them to.

"Excuse me, Evelyn," she said and made a quick decision to go to the ladies' room.

When Jasmine walked out of the ladies' room a few minutes later she felt she was caught in a trap. There was no way she would be able to talk to Wesley alone beforehand. He was standing a few feet away in a group with her father, stepmother and stepsisters, Dr.

Duncan, Paul Sanders, Harold, Miranda and Abraham Danforth.

She felt an overwhelming desire to bolt and go back to the ladies' room but at that moment, Wesley lifted his gaze to hers. Slowly, everyone else's attention became focused on her.

Wesley had always thought Jasmine was the most beautiful woman he had ever seen and tonight he knew without a doubt that she was. The royal blue gown she was wearing looked as if it had been specifically designed just for her body; a body he was getting to know rather well.

"Good evening, everyone," Jasmine said.

As soon as she had spoken, Wesley left the Danforths' side as a smile tilted the corner of his lips. He walked straight over to Jasmine and brushed a kiss on her lips. "Good evening to you, sweetheart. I saw you when I first arrived and wondered where you had gone. I tried calling you earlier today to let you know I was on my way back to Savannah but couldn't reach you."

The entire group got quiet and it was Dr. Carmody who cleared his throat as a lazy smile swept across his face. "I take it that the two of you know each other?" he asked chuckling.

With his hands placed at Jasmine's waist, Wesley turned to her father. "Yes, we do, Dr. Carmody. Jasmine and I have been seeing each other now for a few weeks." He then proceeded to introduce her to the Danforths.

Miranda Danforth smiled. "So this is the woman

you told us about?'' she asked Wesley beaming brightly.

Wesley smiled. ''Yes, she's the one.''

''But—but that's impossible,'' Evelyn Carmody stuttered. She was both surprised and angry and both emotions clearly showed in her features. ''Everyone knows that Jasmine is too wrapped up in her job to take time to see anyone.''

Wesley chuckled as he brought Jasmine closer to his side. ''Then that's all the more reason I should feel special since she's made it a point to take time out of her busy schedule to see me.''

''But she's a newspaper reporter,'' Mallory said with a deliberate sneer, like Jasmine's occupation was the lowest of lows.

Wesley felt Jasmine stiffen beside him and knew she was about to put Mallory in her place but decided he wanted to do the honor. ''Yes, she's a reporter and from the articles I've read that she's written, I think that she's a very good one.'' After taking a sip of his wine he asked, ''And what do you do for a living, Ms. Carmody?''

It was evident that Mallory had been put on the spot with his question. ''I—I don't work,'' she said quietly.

Wesley lifted a brow and said coolly. ''Oh.'' He then turned his attention back to Jasmine. ''Would you care to dance?'' he asked. He wanted to take her away and hold her in his arms. He had missed her like hell over the past few days.

''Have you forgotten, Mr. Brooks, that you promised to dance with me?'' Alyssa said silkily, releasing her hand from Paul Sanders's arm and stepping forward. The look she gave Jasmine was cold and calculating and didn't go unnoticed by Wesley.

He smiled. "Did I? I don't remember making such a promise. I do recall *you* asking me if I would dance with you but I didn't say one way or the other that I would."

Three faces gaped at Wesley in disbelief that he would outright say such a thing. He was making it clear in plain English, that he could be callous and ruthless when he wanted to be and that he would not tolerate Evelyn and her daughters' manipulations. If they kept it up it would only embarrass them because he was not a tolerant man and had no intentions of putting up with their foolishness.

"Oh, sorry my mistake," Alyssa said, returning to her place beside Paul.

Jasmine started to make a smart retort but quickly decided Alyssa and Mallory had definitely been embarrassed enough. She glanced over at her father and saw the tightening of his chin. Evidently tonight had been an eye-opener for him.

Wesley moved closer to Jasmine. "I was supposed to be Jasmine's date tonight, so naturally I plan to spend most of my time dancing with her. Trust me when I say the majority of my attention will be focused mainly on her," he said, meeting Jasmine's gaze and letting everyone know that he meant everything he'd said.

Evelyn couldn't leave well enough alone and said, "Do you think it's wise for a man of your caliber to put all his eggs in one basket, Mr. Brooks?"

Jasmine responded before Wesley had a chance to

do so. She was fed up with her stepmother and step-sisters' insults. "Yes, because a smart man knows a good thing when he sees it. Now please excuse us." She then let Wesley lead her to the dance floor but not before hearing an angry Dr. Carmody tell his wife and stepdaughters he needed to speak with them privately.

Soft strains of music drifted around them as Wesley took Jasmine into his arms as his gaze scanned her features. Everything about her was exquisite. Neither of her stepsisters held a light to her. "You look beau-tiful tonight, Jasmine."

She felt the gentle touch of his fingers on her bare back and shivered at his touch. She tipped her head to meet his gaze. "Thank you. I'm sorry that you got caught up in my stepmother and stepsisters' mischief. I wanted to warn you about Alyssa after Evelyn told me of her interest in you. When it comes to getting what she wants, Alyssa can be totally ruthless."

He shrugged. "I meant everything I said a few mo-ments ago. All my attention is focused on you. And I hate to say it but Evelyn and her daughters may have gone a little too far and I think you father intends to let them know it."

Jasmine thought that very same thing. She stared up at Wesley, drawing in a tremulous breath, wanting to put the episode with Evelyn, Mallory and Alyssa be-hind her. "I'm glad I came tonight, Wes. I missed you."

Wesley smiled, glad to hear her say that because he had missed her, as well. During the day when his mind should have been focused on business, she would creep into his thoughts. And then, at night, he dreamed of her. "I missed you, too. I can't wait to take you home later."

Jasmine lifted a brow. "I drove my own car here tonight."

Wesley's smile widened. "That's fine. We can come back for it tomorrow."

Jasmine nodded and went willingly when he pulled her closer. When the music stopped, it was apparent that Wesley was going to keep her on the dance floor for the next number when she saw Simon Duncan walk up behind him and tap him on the shoulder.

"I believe this is my dance, Mr. Brooks. Ms. Carmody promised it to me earlier, before you arrived."

Wesley lifted a brow and looked at Dr. Duncan before glancing at her. "All right. But I intend to reclaim her as soon as the dance is over," he said, not smiling.

As Dr. Duncan took Jasmine's hand for the next dance, she watched as Wesley walked away.

A few hours later, the door to Wesley's home closed with a soft click and he turned the lock. For long moments he stood there braced against the door as he watched Jasmine move about in his home.

"I thought tonight's affair was wonderful," Jasmine said, turning to him.

"Mmm," he agreed.

"And I thought Dad was most deserving of the award he received tonight. He is such a dedicated physician."

"Mmm," he agreed again.

"And I thought it was perfectly acceptable to dance with Dr. Duncan since I had promised him a dance."

Wesley lifted a brow. On that he would not agree. He had been possessive all night, territorial, and hadn't liked it one damn bit when Simon Duncan had come to claim Jasmine for a dance. She knew he hadn't liked it, which was probably the reason she was bringing it up now. Normally, he was not the jealous type but when it came to Jasmine, he could easily turn green.

When he didn't answer, she asked, "Why did you bring me here instead of taking me home?"

He met her gaze. "I think my reasons would be obvious."

She lifted a chin, not liking the mood he was in. Ever since her dance with Dr. Duncan he had seemed upset. He had no reason to be upset and if he could get angry over something so ridiculous, then so could she. "Your reasons aren't obvious."

She watched as he uncrossed his arms and sighed. "Then I'll make things clearer." He took a step toward her.

She took a step back. "I don't like the way you're acting, Wes."

He noted the contrast between her words and her tone of voice. She was saying one thing but was feeling another. "Then in addition to making things clearer, it seems I also need to change your mind," he said.

Jasmine's breath caught as he began walking toward her. She took another step back. "I don't think that's a good idea," she said softly, tipping her head back when he came to a stop in front of her.

He smiled wondering if she realized she was setting her head and mouth in perfect position for his kiss. "I happen to think it's the best idea I've had all night. And as far as the way you think I'm acting, the only excuse I can come up with is that I didn't like Duncan dancing with you. It bothered the hell out of me and I'm usually not the jealous type. But I was extremely jealous tonight, Jasmine.''

Wesley studied her face, feature by feature, and he recognized the violent desire slamming though his body, as well as the sharp claws of jealousy. What he'd just said was true. He couldn't remember ever being so territorial when it came to a woman; not even for Caroline Perry, the woman he had once loved.

Reaching out, he placed his hands at her waist and claimed her mouth in a smoldering, deep kiss. He felt her resistance ease and she began kissing him back with everything she had inside of her. The pressure of his arms around her increased as he took her mouth hungrily, with earth-shattering greed. He swept her into his arms and headed up the stairs to his bedroom.

After placing her in the middle of his bed, he stood back and began removing his clothes. "You are beautiful," he said, tossing his shirt aside. "There were a lot of men looking at you tonight. Do you know how territorial I felt? But then at the same time, I was proud that you share my bed and not theirs. And tonight, my bed is where I wanted you to be. That's the reason I brought you here instead of taking you home."

He watched as she drew in a shaky breath and lay back in his bed. With an effort that was almost painful, he unzipped his pants and began dragging them down his aroused body. "All I could think about tonight was bringing you here, putting you in my bed, making love to you and driving us both insane.''

After putting on a condom he slowly moved over to the bed. ''I love this gown on you, but I'm going to love it off you even more,'' he said, leaning over and slowly peeling it from her body. With the dress gone, his gaze took in her thigh-high hose, strapless black-laced bra and thong.

Hell, he thought, and all the desire that had accumulated during the evening ripped through him. Although she was perfect, he felt that one thing was missing.

He took a couple of steps over to the nightstand and pulled out another condom package, as well as her locket. Returning to the bed, he gently pulled her up to him and unsnapped her bra before placing the locket around her neck. ''I think it's time I returned this to you,'' he said huskily, and watched how the locket lay between her bare breasts.

''Thank you,'' Jasmine said softly. She met his gaze and when he held out his hand to her, she lifted her hand and placed it in his. He pulled her up into his arms and carried her from the bed toward a wingback chair in the room.

He sat down and placed her to stand between his spread knees. His hands slowly, yet thoroughly skimmed her hips, legs and thighs while easing the thigh-high hosiery down her legs.

''I need to taste you, sweetheart,'' he murmured silkily. Leaning forward his lips touched the bare skin above the waistband of her thong. He felt her shudder and knees weaken and grabbed hold of her hips to hold her steady as he continued to stroke his tongue across her stomach.

He heard her inhale sharply when he slowly eased the thong down her legs as an aching need to taste her consumed him and he lowered his mouth to her middle.

"Oh, Wes," she said digging into his shoulders, her lips emitting incoherent words of pleasure.

He tightened his hand on her thighs as his tongue delved into her flesh, stroking and tasting her over and over again. And when he felt her body beginning to explode, he quickly sat her in his lap, slipping into her, penetrating deep, consuming her and making her completely his.

Consumed with the same urgency that drove Wesley, Jasmine lifted her hips above his and moved over him again and again, mimicking the thrusting motion he was using with his tongue to kiss her. And when she felt him cup the fullness of her breasts in his hands, her body erupted in an explosion that rippled from the top of her head to the soles of her feet.

Wesley shouted her name and then she felt him shudder uncontrollably. She locked her body to his and together they quivered from the force of the climax that tore through them. She heard his growl of pleasure in her ear and at that moment she knew she would always love him.

Ten

Jasmine leaned back in the chair behind her desk as she glanced over the notes she had made on Jake and Larissa Danforth. At the time she had gotten wind that Larissa's child was Jake Danforth's secret baby, she had been determined to expose the man for being an irresponsible playboy. She felt she had every right to write the story since the entire Danforth family had come under media scrutiny when Abraham had tossed his hat into the senatorial race.

Jake had now married Larissa but Jasmine's boss wasn't willing to let the story die. Manny had called her into his office this morning to let her know if she didn't write it then someone else would. A part of her wanted to talk to Wesley about it but knew when it came to her writing anything about the Danforths, that was one topic they wouldn't agree on.

So here she was writing the article that would appear in Sunday's paper. For months she had tried getting information on someone in the Danforth family and had subsequently fallen in love with one of them. She and Wes had been seeing each other now for almost a month and for the time being she saw no end in sight…not that she wanted things to end, but she was realistic enough to know that nothing lasted forever.

The phone rang on her desk and she quickly picked it up. "Hello."

"Hello, sweetheart, I have some bad news."

Jasmine straightened in her chair when she heard the disappointment in Wes's voice. "What?"

"I'm at the airport. Something came up with that business deal in Dallas and I have to fly out immediately."

"Oh." They had planned to go out to dinner and go to a movie later. "That's fine, I need to work on this article I'm doing anyway. When will you be back?"

"Hopefully by this weekend. My plans are to return to Savannah on Saturday night. How about doing me a big favor?"

"What?"

"Be in my bed when I get back."

A smile touched Jasmine's lips. "I think that can be arranged."

Wes chuckled. "It'll give you the chance to use the key I've given you."

Her smile widened. "Okay." He had given her a key to his place last week but she hadn't used it yet.

"Just make yourself at home."

"Thanks and be safe, Wes."

"You, too."

Jasmine hung up the phone then sat back in the chair and bit her bottom lip. She missed him already. Sighing deeply she picked up her notes on Jake and Larissa and began reading. A few minutes later she placed the last page down on her desk. There was definitely a story to tell and she intended to be the one to tell it.

A few hours later she sat across from Ronnie at dinner. She let Ronnie read a rough draft of the article she had written and was relieved when Ronnie told her she thought she'd done a good job.

"Are you going to tell Wesley about the story, especially since it will appear in Sunday's paper?" Ronnie asked, taking a sip of her wine.

"Yes." She planned to tell him when he got home Saturday night. Manny had also been pleased with the article. She only hoped that Wes wouldn't be upset with her for doing it. Once she explained to him that if she hadn't done it then someone else would have, she hoped he would understand.

"How are things going with you and Wesley, Jazz?"

Jasmine shrugged. She had finally told Ronnie about her and Wes the week before the hospital benefit. She hadn't wanted her best friend's mouth to drop open when she and Wes arrived together. "Okay I guess, but I'm beginning to want more out of our relationship.''

''Have you talked to him about it?''

''No, I keep thinking it's not good to mess up a good thing. We go places together and do things together but I feel something is missing.''

''The love thing?''

Jasmine lifted a brow. ''The love thing?''

''Yes. Go ahead and admit you've fallen head over heels in love with the guy.''

Jasmine smiled. ''All right, I admit it, now what?''

''Now you have a good and long conversation with him to find out what his feelings are for you.''

Jasmine sighed. She had thought about doing that several times but could never make herself do it.

''The two of you spend a lot of time together so I'm sure you don't have a communication problem,'' Ronnie added.

Jasmine shook her head. ''No, we don't.'' They talked a lot. He had shared information about his business with her and she told him about different articles she was working on. He even joined her on Sunday dinners at her father's and Evelyn, Mallory and Alyssa always displayed good behavior. Evidently her father had let them know in no uncertain terms that their rude behavior of her would not be tolerated. The three had even gone so far as to apologize to her for how they had acted the night of the hospital benefit.

She sighed. Ronnie was right. It was time she and Wes had a long talk.

* * *

The warm scent of woman was absorbed by Wesley's nostrils the moment he opened his front door on Saturday night. Closing the door behind him, he placed his briefcase aside and took the stairs two at a time. He hadn't seen Jasmine in four days and he missed her like hell.

As soon as he entered his bedroom, he saw her curled in the middle of his bed asleep.

He felt a familiar tightening around his heart, that was getting harder and harder to fight. He'd thought his ability to love and trust another woman had died after what Caroline had done to him but Jasmine had stirred emotions to life inside of him again.

Every free moment that he had he thought of them together. Their favorite place was by the river, where under the beautiful blue sky he would find peace and contentment in talking to her for hours while listening to the soothing sound of the water. She loved the river as much as he did and together they spent hours connecting in a way he had never connected to a woman before. He'd tried to shrug off his desire for her as just a physical thing. But he was beginning to realize and accept that it was more than physical. It was as emotional as it could get.

He loved her.

His body suddenly began to ache all over with a need to hold her in his arms. Now that he had admitted he loved her, he wanted to hold her, heart to heart. Removing his clothes, he walked over to the bed and gathered her into his arms and kissed her awake.

"Wes," she murmured sleepily against his lips. "You're home."

"Yes, baby, I'm home," he said, pushing the covers back and easing into bed beside her. He quickly captured her mouth in a long, deep, drugging kiss, wanting her to know how much he had missed her.

Jasmine pulled her mouth away. "Wes, I need to tell you something," she whispered.

"Later, sweetheart," he said, a whisper against her moist lips. "I don't want to talk now. I want for you to go back to sleep while I hold you. We'll talk tomorrow. There's something I need to tell you, too." He wanted to tell her how much he loved her; how much he needed her. Although he hadn't wanted to love her, she had totally captured his heart and he knew that he had truly come home.

Slipping out of bed the next morning, Wesley pulled on his jeans. He glanced at Jasmine, asleep in his bed. That's where she belonged, he thought, every night.

He rubbed sleep from his eyes and felt the need for a cup of coffee. Leaving the bedroom, he quickly moved down the stairs. Deciding to read the newspaper while Jasmine slept, he opened the door and picked it up off his steps. He smiled and thought that his paper carrier had a good throwing arm to be able to toss the paper over the security gate right onto his doorstep.

By the time the coffee was ready and he had poured himself a cup, he sat down at the kitchen table and opened the paper, scanning the first page.

"What the hell?"

His gaze froze on the front page headline, Jacob Danforth's Secret Isn't A Secret Any Longer.

Wesley drew in a deep breath and tightly clenched his teeth, not believing his eyes when he saw that Jasmine had written the article. He suddenly felt a knife twisting in his heart as he threw the paper down. He had trusted her, fallen in love with her and in the end she had done the same thing Caroline had done to him. She had used him, taken that trust and thrown it right back in his face.

Picking up the paper, he left the kitchen and angrily took the stairs two at a time. A woman had made a fool out of him for the last time.

Jasmine slowly came awake when she inhaled the aroma of brewing coffee. She shifted in bed and smiled thinking that last night was the first time she and Wes had shared a bed and not made love. Evidently he had been as tired as she had.

She glanced up when she heard him enter the room. The smile on her face suddenly fading when she saw his features were ablaze with anger. She sat up. "Wes, what is it?"

When he held the paper out in front of him she knew. "I can explain."

He came into the room. "Can you? How in the hell can you explain disloyalty, Jasmine? Misplaced trust? How can you explain throwing trust back in my face? I thought you had killed that story."

She shook her head. "I had to write it, Wes. If I

hadn't written it, somebody else would have. Read it, Wes, it's not what you think.''

''You used me to betray my best friend and for that I will never forgive you. I thought you were different.

Jasmine had to make him understand. ''Wes, you don't understand. I—''

''I don't want to hear a damn thing you have to say. I want you to get out and take everything of yours with you. When I return I don't want anything in my house to remind me that you've ever been here, and leave my key on my dresser. If you set foot on my property again I will have you arrested, and if you ever go near another Danforth, you'll regret the day you were born.''

He left slamming the door behind him. He was angry, torn up inside, madder than hell. He had to leave. He didn't want to be under the same roof with her. Going into his garage he went straight to his Corvette.

As soon as he pulled out of his driveway, he punched Jake's phone number into his cell phone. He had a lot of explaining to do. He had allowed Jasmine to get close to him, to his family, to the people he cared the most about.

He sighed when Jake didn't answer the phone. Wesley wondered if next Sunday's paper would be running the story about the threatening e-mails Abraham had received. He felt an ache deep down in his gut as pain twisted his insides when he thought of how much he had loved and trusted her.

After driving around for over an hour, with no particular destination in mind, he finally pulled into Jake's driveway, glad to see Jake's car parked there. Cutting off the engine to his Corvette he got out of the car and walked up to the door. Jake opened the door on the first knock.

"Wes? What got you up and out so early?"

From Jake's cheery expression Wesley could only assume he hadn't read the morning's paper. "I called earlier but no one picked up," Wesley said, entering the house when Jake moved aside.

Jake chuckled. "Sunday is one of the few days Peter doesn't wake up at the crack of dawn, so Larissa and I always turn the phones off to get in a little daddy and mommy time. If you get my meaning."

Wesley nodded. He did. "I didn't mean to disturb you and Larissa."

Jake smiled. "You're not disturbing us. But had you come a few hours earlier, I wouldn't been able to say that," he said grinning. "Come on into the kitchen. Larissa is fixing breakfast."

"Good, I need to talk to the two of you."

Larissa turned from the sink when Jake and Wesley walked in the kitchen. Her blue eyes lit into a smile. "Wes, you're just in time for breakfast."

"Thanks." Wesley glanced around. "Where's Peter?"

"He's still asleep," Jake said. "He spent some time with Kim and Zack yesterday and instead of him wearing them out, they wore him out."

Jake and Wesley sat down at the table. "I'm the bearer of bad news this morning," Wesley said with disgust in his voice.

Larissa came to stand next to Jake. Concern etched on her face, as well as on Jake's. "Why? What happened?" Jake asked, placing an arm around his wife's waist.

Wesley sighed deeply. "Jasmine wrote an article that appeared in this morning's paper."

Jake nodded. "Yes? What about it?"

"It's about you, Larissa and Peter," Wes replied.

Larissa smiled. "Yes, we know."

Wesley met Larissa's gaze. "So you've read it?"

Larissa nodded. "Yes, we both did this morning, but I'd already gotten an inside scoop earlier this week when Jasmine gave me a copy of it."

Wesley blinked, more than sure he hadn't heard correctly. "Whoa, back up, time-out. What do you mean Jasmine gave you a copy?"

Larissa's smile widened. "She gave me a copy of the article this week when we had lunch together."

Wesley's brow lifted in surprise. "You and Jasmine had lunch together?"

"Yes, while you were away in Dallas. She wanted to explain why she was doing the article. Her boss was leaning on her to do it and she knew if she didn't do it he would assign someone else to write it."

Wesley leaned back in his chair. "And you accepted that?"

"Yes," Larissa said, cheerfully.

"And we think she did a great job on the article, Wes," Jake added.

"You do?" Wesley asked, completely surprised.

"Yes. Don't you?" Jake responded, studying him intently.

"I haven't read it," Wes admitted.

"Then you should. Larissa and I appreciate the way she wrote it."

Wes suddenly found a cup of coffee shoved in his hand and the newspaper article placed under his nose. "You need to read it, Wes, before you go giving her hell about it," Larissa said.

Wes rubbed a hand over his face. "Too late."

He then took a sip of coffee and began reading the article. Five minutes later he knew that he owed Jasmine a big apology. The article was a feel-good piece that featured Jacob and Larissa as a couple who had found true love and happiness in a reunion romance.

He stood. "I have to get back to my place before Jasmine leaves. I said a lot of mean and nasty things to her," he told them as he headed toward the door.

"Tell her thanks for us," Jake said, pulling his wife into his arms. "Everything she said in that article is true. Larissa and I have found happily ever after."

Wesley nodded as he opened the door and closed it behind him.

When Wesley got back home Jasmine was gone and so were all traces of her…just like he'd asked. He tried calling her at home and didn't get an answer but decided to go over there anyway.

When he got to her apartment he noticed her car missing and since he still had her key he opened her door and let himself in. The house was dark and shut

up like she hadn't been home yet. He wondered if
perhaps she had gone to her father's house. Moments
later he walked out of the house and closed the door
behind him and got back into his car.

Less than thirty minutes later he was ringing her
father's doorbell and was glad when Dr. Carmody answered, smiling. "Wes, this is a pleasant surprise."

"Yes, sir. I was looking for Jasmine and wondered
if perhaps she was here or if you've heard from her."

"No, she isn't here but I did hear from her over an
hour ago. She called to let me know she wasn't coming to dinner and was going out of town for a few
days."

Wesley raised a brow. "Out of town?"

"Yes, she said she needed to get away but didn't
say where she was going."

Wesley nodded, then after a few minutes he said.
"We had an argument."

Dr. Carmody nodded. "But I'm sure it's not anything that can't be repaired."

Wesley nodded again. He wanted to believe that.
"Thanks for the information, sir, and if she calls back,
please tell her to contact me. I need to talk to her."

"Yes, son, I'll most certainly do that."

Dr. Carmody watched as Wesley got back into his
car and drove off.

Wesley spent most of the day by the phone hoping
that Jasmine would call him. Although he didn't hear
from her, he did hear from a number of people in his
family, including Abraham, telling him what a wonderful job she'd done on the article.

Ian had dropped by to bring him up to date on some things that had gone on while he'd been away in Dallas. According to Ian, Abraham's security expert was working diligently behind the scenes trying to find out who had sent those threatening e-mails. Also, a message had been left on Ian's answering machine that Sonny Hernandez wanted to meet with him next week. Ian intended for his answer to be the same as before.

Wesley had tried listening to what Ian was saying but found he was distracted with thoughts of Jasmine. When there had been a lag in their conversation, he'd glanced up to find Ian studying him intently. He filled Ian in on what was going on with him and Jasmine, as well as all the unforgivable things he had said to her.

"I hope you find her and straighten things out, Wes. You're the last person I thought would fall in love with anyone, especially after that Caroline Perry incident and I have to say that I'm truly happy for you."

Wesley nodded. He would be truly happy for himself if he could find Jasmine and straighten out the mess he'd made. "Beware, Ian. If love can find me again then it can definitely find you."

A frown covered Ian's face. "Like hell it will. I don't ever plan on falling in love again."

Wesley chuckled. "Yeah, I thought the same thing."

After Ian had left, Wesley decided to go to Jasmine's apartment again, hoping that perhaps she had changed her mind about going out of town. All the way over to her place, he kept wishing he had read the article before going off on her the way he had. He had claimed he trusted her—what a joke. What kind of trust was that? After everything that he had said, she probably didn't want to ever see him again.

When he didn't find her at home for the second time, he decided to call her office at the newspaper. They confirmed that she'd called earlier that day to request a few days off and wouldn't be back to work until Wednesday. When he'd asked to speak with her friend Ronnie whom he'd met the night of the hospital benefit he was told she was out of town for a week on an assignment.

He knew he had a big job ahead of him when she did return to town. Somehow he had to get her to forgive him and convince her that he loved her and that he had been wrong to think the worst.

He had to find a way to make her see the two of them were meant to be together.

Eleven
———

"**W**elcome back, Jasmine."

Jasmine smiled at Brad whose desk was right next to hers. "Thanks."

"And that was a nice article you did last Sunday on Jacob and Larissa Danforth," he added.

She nodded. "Thanks, again."

Evidently picking up on the fact that she wasn't in a talkative mood, Brad turned back to his computer and resumed typing. Jasmine sighed, regretting her solemn mood and hoping she wouldn't cry again. Over the past three days that was all she'd done.

She had needed time alone and had decided to get away. After packing up all her stuff in Wesley's house she had decided to take the hour drive to Fernandina Beach, Florida. She had checked into a hotel on the beach and stayed mainly in her hotel room. She had not wanted any contact with the outside world.

She had tried to eradicate Wesley from her mind, as well as her heart.

Of course she had done a poor job of it. Love wasn't supposed to hurt this way but it did and she wanted none of it. She understood that he'd been hurt in college, but it had been unfair for him to group her and Caroline Perry in the same category.

Not wanting to think about Wesley any longer, she thought of the conversation she'd had with her father earlier that morning. He had called and invited her to meet him for breakfast. It was then that he'd told her of his decision to divorce Evelyn. He'd confided that he wasn't happy with his marriage and hadn't been for quite some time. He felt it was time to bring things to an end. He had planned to see his attorney later that day to file the papers and intended to give Evelyn what he considered a generous divorce settlement. A part of Jasmine truly regretted things had ended that way.

She looked up, startled, when Polly, the staff secretary, set a huge vase of fresh-cut flowers in front of her.

"This was just delivered to you, Jazz. It's a beautiful arrangement. Whoever he is, you might want to think about keeping him around," the perky woman said before walking off.

Jasmine noticed the delivery had gotten Brad's and a couple of the other reporters' attention. As calmly as she could, she pulled off the card and read it. There were two words: *I'm sorry.*

Jasmine breathed deeply. Although the card had not

been signed she had a good idea who had sent the flowers. Deciding she didn't want to deal with Wes's apology at the moment, she opened her desk drawer and placed the card inside.

Less than thirty minutes later Polly came back to her desk with another arrangement of flowers, this time a dozen red roses. "This guy is pretty serious," Polly said, sitting the flowers next to the other arrangement. "I know I would keep him around," she added.

As soon as Polly walked off, Jasmine quickly pulled off the card and read it: *I love you.*

Her breath caught in her throat. "Since when?" she couldn't help asking herself angrily out loud.

"Since the first moment I saw you."

Jasmine turned around to find Wes standing beside her desk. "What are you doing here?" she asked barely able to catch her breath.

"I'm here to see you and to make amends."

She noticed her co-workers' curious stares and wondered where Security was when you needed them. "I got the flowers and want to thank you but we don't have anything to say to each other, Wes."

"You may have nothing to say to me but I have a lot to say to you."

She frowned, again noticing her co-workers' attention. "I don't want to listen, Wes, and this is not the time or the place."

He leaned against her desk. "For us any time is the right time and any place is the right place."

Her face turned a darker brown when she suddenly remembered how they'd made love any time and practically any place over the past month. "I'd rather not talk about it."

"But I want to talk about it. I owe you an apology and I want to say that I'm sorry, right here and right now. I misjudged you because of my experience with another reporter back in college and I had no right to do that. I'm truly sorry, Jasmine."

Jasmine frowned. "Great, you're sorry. Now can I get back to work?"

"And I love you, Jasmine."

Jasmine closed her eyes and inhaled a deep breath. Telling her that he was sorry was one thing but telling her that he loved her was another. "No, you don't."

"Yes, I do. That's the reason I hurt so bad when I thought you had betrayed me. If I hadn't loved you so much, I would not have gotten as mad as I did. I love you, Jasmine. I love you and I want to marry you. I want to spend the rest of my life proving that I am worthy of your love."

Tears streamed down Jasmine's face. She couldn't help but notice the entire office had stopped working and was watching the two of them. Even Manny had come out of his office to see what was going on.

At that moment the reader board that was hooked up to the wire service began beeping and everyone turned to read the message that was boldly blinking.

Wesley Brooks loves Jasmine Carmody
and is asking for her hand in marriage.

Jasmine turned and met Wes's gaze, wondering how he had arranged that, then decided Wesley

Brooks could do just about anything, even capture her heart.

In front of her and everyone in her office who were looking on, he got down on his knees and took her hand in his. ''I love you, Jasmine, and more than anything I want you to be my wife. Will you marry me?''

Jasmine wiped the tears from her eyes. She knew that Wes was a very private person and it had taken a lot for him to come down to the newsroom to make not only a public apology but a public proposal, as well. She loved him and was convinced that he loved her.

''I love you, too, and yes, Wes, I'll marry you.''

Cheers went up and everyone applauded. Wes placed a huge diamond ring on Jasmine's finger before pulling her into his arms, sealing her answer with a kiss.

Jasmine's heart overflowed with love and she knew at that moment that she was the luckiest woman in the world.

Later that night Jasmine lay in Wesley's arms while she slept completely naked, except for the locket around her neck and the new engagement ring on her finger.

Wesley drew a deep, calming breath as he studied the peaceful look on Jasmine's face. His hand gently caressed her stomach. Visions of her pregnant suddenly filled his mind.

Becoming a father was something that he had never thought about before. He had been in awe at how easily Jake had stepped into the role of father. He knew his best friend loved his son to distraction, even though a year ago the last thing on Jake's mind was having an immediate family. Now Jake looked like he wouldn't think of having it any other way.

Being careful not to wake her, he slid his arms around Jasmine and brought her closer to him, needing the bodily contact. He'd come so close to losing her.

Suddenly she stirred in his arms and her eyes opened. "You're awake," he said softly.

At the sound of Wesley's husky voice she glanced over at him. His smile was warm, seductive. His gaze had moved from her face to the nipples of her exposed breasts. "Yes, I'm awake."

His hazel eyes returned to her face. "Good."

He moved his body over hers and took her mouth. Her body trembled and she knew the love they had would last a lifetime. He broke off the kiss and held her gaze. She still couldn't believe that he had actually come to the newsroom to apologize and to ask her to marry him.

Another surprise had been the arrangement he'd made with Miranda Danforth. After leaving the newsroom, he had taken her to Harold and Miranda's home where the older woman had a surprise informal dinner party planned with all the Danforths present. Tears had come into Jasmine's eyes when Abraham Danforth gave a touching speech, welcoming her into the Danforth family.

Wesley and Jasmine had decided to plan a small private wedding on Wesley's property; a section on the Savannah River where he had taken her for picnics several times. It was a special place where they would talk for hours and make love under the beautiful sky. The river held special memories for the both of them and they felt it would be the ideal place to pledge their lives together.

"I love you," Wesley whispered softly.

"I love you, too."

Earlier when they had arrived at his home, before making love to her, he had held her tenderly in his arms and told her the entire story of Caroline Perry and how the woman's betrayal had made him leery of falling in love again—especially with another reporter.

She had understood and had tried kissing away all the pain that Caroline Perry had ever caused him.

"No regrets?" he asked with their gazes still locked.

She shook her head. "None."

"What about your desire to write that 'big story'?" he asked quietly.

Jasmine thought about his question a while before answering. "In a way that article on Jake and Larissa *was* my big story. I've gotten a lot of positive feedback about it and I found out it's not what story you write, but rather how you write the story." And to think she had once been so hell-bent on bringing the Danforth family down. But that was before a certain person in that family had stolen a place in her heart.

"Everyone is right you know," he said reclaiming her thoughts. "You did a wonderful job on that article. Jake and Larissa are as much in love as you said they were." He pulled her closer to him, wanting to make love to her again.

Jasmine smiled. "I know. That's why I felt that I

had to be the one to write the story to do it justice. Whenever I see them I think of love."

"And what do you think about when you see us?" Wesley asked her.

She met his gaze and smiled. "I think of passion, love and happiness." She shifted in his arms. "What do you think about when you see us?"

Wesley chuckled. "I see a man who met his match, a man who found his soul mate."

Jasmine's smile widened. "Is that good?"

Wesley leaned over and before covering her mouth with his, he whispered huskily, "I can't think of anything better."

*   *   *   *   *

Watch for the next book in Silhouette Desire's
DYNASTIES: THE DANFORTHS,
THE BOSS MAN'S FORTUNE
by Kathryn Jensen, available in May 2004.

And out this month, look for
Brenda Jackson's THE MIDNIGHT HOUR
from St. Martin's Press.

The captivating family saga of the Danforths continues with

THE BOSS MAN'S FORTUNE

by

Kathryn Jensen

(Silhouette Desire #1579)

Errant heiress Katie Fortune had left home and her
oppressive lifestyle behind and began anew—as secretary
to Ian Danforth. The renowned playboy was a genius
in the boardroom. But it was his bedroom manner
that Katie couldn't stop fantasizing about....

DYNASTIES : THE DANFORTHS

**A family of prominence...
tested by scandal, sustained by passion!**

Available May 2004 at your favorite retail outlet.

If you enjoyed what you just read,
then we've got an offer you can't resist!

Take 2 bestselling love stories FREE!

Plus get a FREE surprise gift!

Clip this page and mail it to Silhouette Reader Service™

IN U.S.A.
3010 Walden Ave.
P.O. Box 1867
Buffalo, N.Y. 14240-1867

IN CANADA
P.O. Box 609
Fort Erie, Ontario
L2A 5X3

YES! Please send me 2 free Silhouette Desire® novels and my free surprise gift. After receiving them, if I don't wish to receive anymore, I can return the shipping statement marked cancel. If I don't cancel, I will receive 6 brand-new novels every month, before they're available in stores! In the U.S.A., bill me at the bargain price of $3.57 plus 25¢ shipping and handling per book and applicable sales tax, if any*. In Canada, bill me at the bargain price of $4.24 plus 25¢ shipping and handling per book and applicable taxes**. That's the complete price and a savings of at least 10% off the cover prices—what a great deal! I understand that accepting the 2 free books and gift places me under no obligation ever to buy any books. I can always return a shipment and cancel at any time. Even if I never buy another book from Silhouette, the 2 free books and gift are mine to keep forever.

225 SDN DNUP
326 SDN DNUQ

Name	(PLEASE PRINT)	
Address	Apt.#	
City	State/Prov.	Zip/Postal Code

* Terms and prices subject to change without notice. Sales tax applicable in N.Y.
** Canadian residents will be charged applicable provincial taxes and GST.
All orders subject to approval. Offer limited to one per household and not valid to current Silhouette Desire® subscribers.
® are registered trademarks of Harlequin Books S.A., used under license.

DES02   ©1998 Harlequin Enterprises Limited

COMING NEXT MONTH

#1579 THE BOSS MAN'S FORTUNE—Kathryn Jensen
Dynasties: The Danforths
Errant heiress Katie Fortune had left home and her oppressive lifestyle
behind and began anew—as secretary to Ian Danforth. The renowned
playboy was a genius in the boardroom. But it was his bedroom
manner that Katie couldn't stop fantasizing about….

#1580 THE LAST GOOD MAN IN TEXAS—Peggy Moreland
The Tanners of Texas
She'd come to Tanner's Crossing looking for her family. What
Macy Keller found was Rory Tanner, unapologetic ladies' man. Rory
agreed to help with Macy's search—to keep an eye on her. But as the
sexual tension began to hum between them, it became difficult to keep
his *hands* off her!

#1581 SHUT UP AND KISS ME—Sara Orwig
Stallion Pass: Texas Knights
Sexy lawyer Savannah Clay was unlike any woman he'd ever known.
Mike Remington hadn't believed she'd take him up on his marriage
proposal—if only for the sake of the baby he'd inherited. Falling into
bed with the feisty blonde was inevitable; it was falling in love that
Mike was worried about….

#1582 REDWOLF'S WOMAN—Laura Wright
When Ava Thompson had left Paradise, Texas, four years ago, she'd
carried with her a little secret. But her daughter was not so little
anymore. Unsuspecting dad Jared Redwolf was blindsided by the
truth—and shaken by the power Ava had over him still. Could the
passion they shared see them through?

#1583 STORM OF SEDUCTION—Cindy Gerard
Tonya Griffin was a photographer of the highest repute…and
Web Tyler wanted her work to grace the pages of his new magazine.
But Web also had other plans for the earthy beauty…and they didn't
involve work, but the most sensual pleasures.

#1584 AT ANY PRICE—Margaret Allison
Kate Devonworth had a little problem. Her small-town paper needed
a big-time loan, and her childhood crush turned wealthy investor
Jack Reilly was just the man to help. Kate resolved to keep things
between them strictly business…until she saw the look in his eyes.
A look that matched the desire inside her….

SDCNM0404